EVENING SON

A NOVEL

STUART FABE

Evening Son

Copyright 2019 by Stuart A. Fabe

All Rights Reserved

No part of this publication can be reproduced, stored in a retrieval system, or transmitted, in any form or by any means— electronic, mechanical, photo-reproductive, recording, or otherwise— without prior written permission by the publisher, except for the inclusion of brief quotations in a review.

For more information about this title or to order other books, contact the publisher:

Stuart A. Fabe
Greencastle, Indiana
stuartfabe@gmail.com

ISBN: 978-0-692-04105-5

Printed in the United States

Author's Note

THERE'S SOMETHING deeply personal about my attraction to the north woods of North America. Whether that pristine north is in the United States or Canada, I'm drawn to its tea-stained streams and glacial lakes, its towering maples, birches, and pines, and the wildlife that calls this spectacular geography home.

Fifty years ago I spent the first of two summers as a camp counselor at a fine boys' camp in Northern Wisconsin close to the clear waters of the Bois Brule River. Those summers imbued me with a sense of wonder and belonging. For these compelling reasons, I decided to make the environs of Douglas County, Wisconsin, the setting for this novel.

Evening Son is the fourth story in my Clay Arnold series and is intended to show the evolution of my main character, Clay, and my own growth as

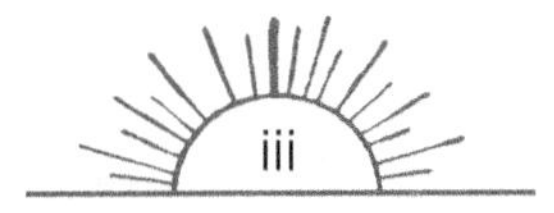

a writer. Clay is now a husband and the father of his and Maggie's nine-year-old son, Bodie. As in life, a person's focus sometimes changes, and Clay's role as a family man provides new dimensions to how he faces conflict, and how he helps guide his son in dealing with the inevitable struggles of life.

As in all of my stories, there are aspects that are well grounded in facts while many others that are the creation of my imagination. I'm a storyteller after all. I sincerely hope you enjoy reading *Evening Son* as much as I've reveled in letting my mind navigate the rapids, eddies, and pools of an ever-flowing stream of consciousness.

Stuart Fabe

Dedication

To the voyagers of the Bois Brule River,
past, present, and future,
who paddle its waters and
respect its wildness as a waterway of life.

And

To the Robert Banks Family of
Douglas County, Wisconsin,
whose enduring friendship to the natural world
transcends generations.

Chapter 1

TIME IS MOVING ON. I feel it in my bones, my marrow, my skin. Time isn't something that I thought much about when I was younger, but now at age forty-five, with a precocious nine-year-old son and an ever-intriguing, forty-something wife, I'm viewing glimpses of my mortality with a more deferential and respectful eye. It's as if Time has its own instincts though. It moves inexorably onward without any care for dawdlers. Rich man, poor man, genius or dullard … Time flows like a river with no regard for one's achievements or station in life. In the end the river of Time witnesses everything and everyone come and go.

My name's Clay Arnold, and I find myself contemplating these mind-bending concepts as I sip from a steamy mug of coffee and lean on the railing of my rooftop deck overlooking the renovated, nineteenth-century beer brewery complex that I own. It's also the place that my family and closest friends call home.

I love spending early mornings here. Most mornings, even during winter, Maggie and I step outside to welcome a new day if only for a few minutes. This morning is far more pleasant than the winter mornings though. It's early June here along the White River in central Indiana just a few miles above Indianapolis. I'm greeted by fully leafed-out trees, birds calling to potential mates, and an orange sun peering over the horizon. It's about six thirty and Maggie and our son, Bodie, are still snug under their blankets.

I take another sip of coffee and can't help but reflect on how much my life has evolved over the past decade. Yes, I'm still a passionate photographer traveling the world on photographic assignments that I find personally appealing. Yes, both Maggie and I have managed to balance our demanding careers with a rock-solid home life, made even stronger with a lot of help from our friends. And yes, I'm still a guy who tries to live a life that contributes to the greater good, but I admit to still feeling possessed by thoughts of exacting harsh justice on anyone who threatens the people I care about or who prey upon the more vulnerable people in our society. Losing my lifelong friend, Weed Rawlins, to a henchman's bullet several years ago sealed that searing sentiment inside me forever. Fortunately, my urges to even the score for those in need have subsided ever since Maggie and I got married nearly ten years ago and brought our bodacious, bright, and uninhibited son into the world. Unfortunately, I know these avenging impulses still reside within me, and I've given up trying to fully suppress them. I'm a loving husband, father, and friend, but I'll be the first to admit that I'm not a perfect guy.

As I look across the courtyard of the brewery complex, I see my close friend, Mace Davis, step outside of the old power plant where he lives alone now that our adopted son, Rennie Cotton, is away at college. Our hobbling black Labrador, Lex, stays close to Mace as he putters around our property keeping things in proper order. Both Mace and Lex are now well into their dotage, and a wave of sadness grips me as I see that their footsteps aren't as sure as they once were, and I know that their final days are not too far in the future.

Mace is eighty-plus-years-old now, and while he's still capable of maintaining much of our property as he has done for more than six decades ever since he arrived here looking for work as a skinny fourteen-year-old kid from the Bahamas. Mace is as important to me as any person on the planet, and while we come from very different backgrounds, Mace has been a friend, mentor, and confidante to me as few others have ever been.

Good ol' Lex is a wonderful dog, and I am amazed that he's still viable given that he lost a leg to a gunman's bullet a dozen years ago while protecting Rennie and my lifelong friend, Tori Rawlins. Lex is now fourteen years old, and I sense his end is growing very near. He rarely wanders far from Mace's side now.

From the courtyard below, Mace looks up to my rooftop deck and waves a greeting to me. His broad smile brightens my day as much as the rising sun. I wave back to him and hide the sadness that I feel knowing that my close family of friends will soon be smaller given the unstoppable vagaries of time.

I take another sip from my cooling mug of coffee and see Tori step out onto the porch of the old farmhouse which is situated across the courtyard next to Mace's power plant. Tori has been totally blind since birth and is like a sister to me. I grew up with Tori and her late brother, Weed Rawlins, and another wave of sadness seizes me as I recall Weed dying in my arms from a gunshot wound while we were following clues to find a hidden trove of rare art ten years ago. Besides being "family" to me, Tori and Weed were very popular musicians, and a tear comes to my eye knowing that I'll never see them perform together again. But time moves on, and fortunately Tori found purpose in life by helping to raise young Rennie and prepare him for college. Thankfully, my loving wife, Maggie, and Tori have grown very close, and while the composition of our family has changed over the years, we're all devoted to one another. As Weed used to say, "We stick together!"

I shift my gaze from my friends below and look past the walnut trees to the White River a hundred yards away. The sun's rays have pierced through the trees' foliage, and the river's waters appear silver-white with sunlight attaching itself to streaming molecules of oxygen and hydrogen.

A moment later my solitude is dashed by a flash of fur and whiskers as my old pal, Satchmo, leaps up to the handrail near my arm. Satchmo is the largest darn Maine Coon cat that you ever saw and literally rules the environs of the brewery complex with all of the stealth and physicality of a hungry lion. And while Satchmo is well over thirteen years old now, nary a chipmunk, mole, rat, or mouse has evaded my feline friend. Ever since my son, Bodie, has taken over the responsibilities of feeding and playing with Satchmo, we don't spend as much time together as we once did, but we share a lot of history. I bend my head down to the big cat's face, and he nuzzles my nose and forehead with friendly vigor. In our own ways, we know that we're part of the same pack.

"Well, Satchmo, time is moving on for all of us," I say. "I'm still counting on you keeping our home rodent-free for a lot of years yet." My pal replies to my entreaty by doing what cats do best. He grooms himself for a moment and then bounds away. "Oh well," I breathe out loud.

Alone again, I look in the distance at the White River and think about another stream that captured my heart over thirty-five years ago. The Bois Brule River in Douglas County in Northern Wisconsin is a pristine stream that I first became familiar with as a camper at Camp Voyager on Lake Winneboujou. The Brule River is about fifteen miles from camp, and my fellow campers and I paddled it often over the summers that I spent there. It's totally different from our own White River, but each in its own way is a vital waterway. While the White River has a muddy, mucky bottom accommodating to bass and panfish, the Brule River has a well-oxygenated sandy, gravelly bottom that is perfect for brook, rainbow, and brown trout. Each stream has its charm, but to this day the

Brule River has a magical tug on my memory, and I can't wait to introduce Bodie to its wonders.

I take another sip from my mug and decide to pour the rest of my now cold coffee over the deck and go inside for a fresh, hot refill. As I quietly reenter our bedroom though, I hear a loud sound that I've grown accustomed to: "Daaaddd! Where are you, Dad?!" It's Bodie, and he's awake.

"I'm out here on the deck, Bodie," I hoarsely call back to him. "Your mom's still asleep, so try to keep the noise level down, will ya?!"

"Too late!" I hear Maggie's muffled voice from beneath her pillow. A moment later our bodacious Bodie runs through our bedroom and meets me at the sliding door leading inside. Satchmo is hot on his heels, and the two of them exude all of the blurry excitement of two cats chasing each other.

"Hey, Dad!" Bodie exclaims as he body-slams into my legs. "I was wondering where you were!"

I bend down and give my son a warm hug and can't help but smile at how much he's grown into a fine, young fella who has all of the inhibitions and shyness of a Ninja warrior. Bodie is nine years old now and has a combination of Maggie's beauty and my rugged good looks, and fortunately for him he has more of Maggie's great genes than mine. Like Maggie, he has deep auburn hair and penetrating, laughing green eyes. I adore our little boy and feel so fortunate that he's in our life.

"C'mon!" I say. "Let's make sure Mom's awake!" And at that we both dive onto our bed and crawl under the covers with Maggie.

"Ooooff!" we hear Maggie manage to exhale as we cocoon our bodies next to her warmth.

"Are you awake yet, Mom?" Bodie asks just as Satchmo leaps onto the bed to join in the revelry.

"Gee, Bodie, I may have been a few minutes ago, but I think that's history," Maggie says as she envelops our son in a consuming motherly hug.

"I'm hungry!" Bodie declares. "Want me to make breakfast?"

"Uh sure!" Maggie replies. "Why don't you see if Tori, Mace, and Lex want to join us, okay? Your dad and I will be down in a few minutes."

At that, Bodie throws off his covers and clambers out of our bed. "C'mon Satchie! Let's go round up the rest of the troops!" A moment later they're gone, and Maggie and I lay there with amused expressions on our face.

"How did we get so lucky, Maggie? He's such a terrific kid!"

"I don't know," she replies. "Let's see how his breakfast turns out before we call ourselves lucky," she teases.

I snuggle even closer to Maggie and say, "Now, I know how we can get really lucky," and I proceed to nuzzle her neck.

"Not now, you randy beast!" she chortles back at me. "You know we never know when that kid of ours will rematerialize, plus I'm really hungry too. Perhaps you may get lucky a little later. On the other hand you may not get lucky again until Bodie is off at summer camp."

"I don't think I can wait that long," I pathetically admit, but I've come to know that with a child our moments of intimacy in recent years have had to be strategically planned. Not complaining; just sayin'! Okay, maybe I'm complaining, but I'm trying to be mature about this!

Ten minutes later we descend down the steps and are greeted by Tori, Mace, and good ol' Lex plus a cacophony of kitchen clatter as Bodie assumes a leadership role in making eggs and bacon and toast. Like I said, the lad is definitely bodacious … and a little loud!

"G'morning guys," Maggie says to Tori and Mace. "I hope Bodie didn't wake you two up too early."

"Naw," Mace says. "You know Tori and I are early birds. We've got too much stuff to do around here anyway. Isn't that right, Tori?"

"I'll say!" she agrees. "Especially since Rennie's at school and not around to pick up the slack. Sure could use his help again with our garden. Planting and especially weeding are never-ending tasks."

"I can help you, Aunt Tori," Bodie offers, "at least until I go off to Camp Voyager."

"Tell us again when you're leaving for Wisconsin," Mace says. "I know it's coming up pretty soon."

"In about a week, Uncle Mace," Bodie replies. He looks at me to confirm his departure date, and I offer a suggestion. "You know, Bodie, I've been thinking about something and want to see how you feel about it."

"What is it, Dad?" he asks curiously, and Maggie shoots me a glance of curiosity as well.

"Well, Camp Voyager's season begins in about ten days, and I thought maybe you and I could drive up a few days early, and I could introduce you to fly fishing for trout on the Brule River which is where I learned how to do it when I was about your age."

"Really?!" Bodie replies as he looks over at Maggie to make sure his mom is agreeable too.

"What do you think, Maggie?" I ask hopefully. "Do you mind if the 'bodacious one' and I head north a little early?"

In addition to being a beautiful woman, Maggie is wise beyond her years, especially when she agrees with my suggestions.

"Hmmm," she ponders. "I don't know if I'm ready for my baby to leave me for the summer," she says in half jest.

"I'm not a baby, Mom!" Bodie protests. "Can Dad and I go early, please?!" I enthusiastically nod my head affirmatively in hopes that she's agreeable.

"Hmmm," she says again. "Maybe, but only if your Dad promises me that he'll keep a close eye on you."

"Now what could go wrong?!" I say. "We're only going fishing on the Brule River for a couple of days, and then I'll drop Bodie off at camp. Nothing bad's going to happen. I promise."

At that, Mace and Tori begin rolling their eyes and try to suppress their laughter knowing full well that every time I've said something like that, crazy stuff happens.

"But you know, Bodie, fly fishing is more challenging than other types of fishing, so I think we should spend a few hours on our White River to make sure you get the hang of it. I've got a box of flies and two nice bamboo fly rods that I inherited from your grandfather. One of them is the perfect length for you. Are you game?"

"Heck yeah, Dad!" he replies. "And I'll help Tori in the garden too, and whatever you need help with, Mom. Is it okay if we go early?!"

As I said, Maggie is a wise woman, and she knows that my bonding with our son on a fishing trip to a pristine trout stream borders on the magical for guys regardless of age.

"Yeah, it's okay," she confirms, "but I better get at least one letter from you every week you're gone, mister, and you sir," she says pointing her index finger in my direction, "No unnecessary drama, right?!"

I begin to offer a defensive reply but instead simply say, "Of course, darling! No unnecessary drama. You can count on us, right Bodie?!"

Chapter 2

THE TALL, TRIM, MIDDLE-AGED man stands on the bank of the Bois Brule River just above Cedar Island and visually scans the river and surrounding landscape in all directions. His steel-gray eyes look to the treetops to check wind direction, and he's rewarded by seeing a bald eagle glide and settle into its nest atop a two-hundred-year-old white pine. The man shifts his gaze to the river itself, and he slowly relaxes into a near-meditative state as he closes his eyes and listens to the sounds of the stream and smells the aroma of coniferous pollen mixed with deciduous growth.

"Banks, this is home," he says out loud to himself. "This where I'm meant to be. This is where I can be myself, see the stars at night, paddle this river, and be at peace."

Banks steps into the water up to his knees and feels the gentle current move against his insulated waders. Again, he closes his eyes, calms his breathing, and senses the timelessness of the current. With the sound of the flowing water streaming in his ears, he regards the river's flow as no different than the blood pulsing through his veins. They are one.

He opens his eyes again and spies a submerged rock near the opposite bank. A bush hangs over the water and provides a cool dark haven for a trout. Banks checks the Adams dry fly at the end of his tippet, strips off a couple of feet of line, raises his rod tip, does a couple of false casts to peel off more line, and with the subtle artistry of a symphony conductor, Banks lands his fly in the water just upstream of the bush and submerged rock. The Adams fly remains motionless on the surface for a moment, then begins drifting over the rock, and slowly floats further away. Banks draws in the slack in his fly line and with a relaxed dexterity, he lifts the fly off the water with nary a splash and lands it twenty feet to the left in midstream. Immediately, a small brook trout slams the fly with a dramatic eruption of white-edged fins, a trim colorful body, and a glorious tail.

"C'mon over here, little fella," Banks whispers to the brookie. The trout struggles to free himself with all of his might but soon tires from his exertion. A few moments later Banks holds a twelve-inch brookie in his wet hands.

"Hold still now, my little river prince," he says with calmness. Banks takes his forceps and carefully removes the fly's hook. He gives his new acquaintance one last admiring look and gently slides him out of his hands and back into the stream.

Banks inspects his Adams fly and redresses it to make sure his dry fly stays on the water's surface. He takes a few moments to let the dressing dry, and his mind wanders back to an earlier stage in his life that was nothing like the life he lives now. His arduous military training as a marine and the violent operations that he participated in were all-consuming to him for over a decade. The acrid odor of explosives and the smell of burned buildings, vehicles, and human bodies were memories that he tries to leave in the past. Some memories just never go away though, and were it not for the camaraderie of his fellow marines, and one man in particular, he's not sure that his humanity would've remained intact. He forcefully brushes those haunting thoughts away.

"Those days are over, Banks," he reminds himself aloud. "I did my time. I did what I had to do for my country and the corps. Now it's my time. Breathe, Banks, breathe and let this river heal your spirit."

Banks stands motionless in the Brule River, and he watches the stream's tea-stained waters drift by. Leaves, twigs, and other flotsam float past his field of vision on the Brule's journey some thirty miles downstream to where it empties into Lake Superior. He closes his eyes again to regain his composure after thinking about his career as a marine.

"No more conflict. No more death. That's behind me now," he whispers solemnly to himself. He reopens his eyes and spies the sunken rock and overhanging bush again. "I know you're in there, Mister Trout," he says softly. Given the tight quarters of the surrounding trees, Banks executes a roll cast and lays his redressed fly in the water again just above the rock and bush. It sits placidly there for a moment, and like before, it begins to slowly flow over the rock and drift away.

"Well, my fine-finned friend," he voices, "I guess you're going to make a liar out of me, aren't you?" His Adams fly moves a few feet further downstream away from his intended spot, and all of a sudden the surface of the river erupts with the marauding attack of a large rainbow trout.

"Whoa!" he yelps. "You're a big one, aren't you!" Banks steps a little further into the stream and steadies his feet on the gravelly river bottom and begins the steady retrieve of his fly line. The rainbow moves his large body perpendicular to Banks's position and tries to dive for the safety of the submerged rock. Banks holds his fly line in his left hand and begins bringing the strong fish into midstream and away from the rock. The twenty-inch trout breeches the surface and suspends momentarily in midair.

"Oh yeah!" Banks exhales. "You're a beauty, my friend!"

The struggle ensues for another fifteen long seconds until the great fish is in the angler's net by his thighs. Its mouth is open with the fly imbedded in its wide maw. Banks inspects the size and wondrous colors that give the rainbow trout its apt name. A moment later Banks gently removes the fly with his forceps and lets the trout slip back into the Brule to live another day. Catch-and-release is Banks's fishing motto, very different he thought from his combat life as a killing machine.

Banks steps out of the water and sits on the broad trunk of a fallen maple with a small, self-satisfied smile on his face. "Veni, vidi, vici," he voices in Latin, recalling Julius Caesar's famous words. "I came, I saw, I conquered … and then I safely released you," he ad libs. He closes his eyes again to listen to the rhythm of the stream and permanently saves the recollection of his encounter with the rainbow in his memory.

"Hey, Mr. Banks!" comes a man's voice. "Are you out here?" It's Cedar Island's custodian and chef, Cecil Johns.

"Over here," Banks replies, "And my name's Banks, Cecil; not Mr. Banks, just Banks, okay? I keep telling you that."

"Yessir," comes the other man's voice. " You have a phone call, sir."

"You came all of the way out here to tell me I have a phone call?!" Banks asks incredulously.

"Yessir, Mister, uh, I mean Banks, sir. It's Washington, sir, and the caller said he'd wait on the line for you."

"Well, crap!" Banks replies, "I guess that's the end of today's bliss! Did the caller say what he wanted?"

"Well, I told him you were fishing on the river and asked him if I could give you a message."

"And, what did he say?" Banks prompted.

"Uh, he said 'Oorah brother', and that'd you'd understand, sir, and that he'd hold on the line for you."

Banks closes his eyes again, but his mental connection with the Brule River drifts away like a dry leaf floating out of view.

"I'll be right up to the lodge, Cecil."

Banks walks up the path to the main lodge on Cedar Island and discards his waders and fisherman's vest on the back porch. He props his fly rod on an old wooden chair next to them and walks into the kitchen. He reaches for an old wall phone in the kitchen and says, "This is Banks."

"Yessir, Mr. Banks, this is Roxanne at the White House. President Horvath will be right with you, sir."

"My name's just Banks. No mister, Roxanne. Just Banks, and will you ask him to hurry it along. I've got things I need to do here." Banks couldn't help but smile at the thought of telling her to hurry the president of the United States along. "That'll get his attention," he laughs out loud to himself.

A minute later a familiar voice speaks into the phone, and two old friends connect as only former comrades-in-arms can do. "Is that you, Banks, you old reprobate?!"

"Yeah, Jake, it's good to hear your voice. I hope your secretary didn't wet her drillies when I asked her to hurry you along."

"Naw, Roxanne is made of sterner stuff than that. Hell, you gotta be living in this nutty town. What have you been doing with yourself?"

"Not too much. Pretty much looking after Cedar Island and trying to stay below the radar. Just landed a beautiful twenty-inch rainbow a few minutes ago if that counts for anything."

"Sounds divine to me, Banks. Fishing the Brule with you sure brings back some great memories for me. And, that's the reason for my call, well that and just wanting to hear your snarky-ass voice."

"Oorah that, Jake, so, what's going on? I know you're a pretty busy feller these days."

"Roxanne and I were looking at my schedule, and I see a brief window of free time next week. I was wondering if I could descend on your little piece of paradise on the Brule and spend a couple of days hunting trout with you."

"Sounds like a really good idea to me," Banks replies to him. "You know we're not as fancy as a lot of the places those bigwigs put you up at, but it's clean and private, and I promise you we'll catch fish. Just let me know when you plan to come, and we'll take care of the rest."

"I think you know I don't need fancy accommodations, Banks, especially considering some of the crap holes you and I shared together in the marines. As much as anything I would love ditching Washington for a couple of days and just hanging out with a close friend."

"It's been too long, Jake. I'm delighted that you want to come here. Just bring comfortable clothes. I have all of the fishing gear that you'll need."

"Thanks, Banks, I need a break. Roxanne will get back in touch with you shortly with my travel plans, plus you know my Secret Service detail will want to arrive a day or so before me to do whatever they need to do. You can expect a rather sober fellow named Hank Splinter to show up to handle the advance security stuff. He isn't a lot of laughs, but I guess you and I weren't either when we were in uniform."

"Copy that, Jake. Get yourself out of DC and come to northern Wisconsin. We'll be ready whenever you get here, my friend."

Chapter 3

"DAADDD! WHERE ARE YOU, Dad?!" Bodie hollers as he and Satchmo come running down the steps from his bedroom to the main floor of our home looking for me. "Daaddd!"

From our antique camera museum next door, Mace and I can hear the bodacious one bellowing through the walls.

"That lad has some serious lungs on him," Mace states with a look of amusement on his face.

"Tell me about it!" I deadpan. "I love the little fella, but he can sure foul up the quiet karma of the place with the best of 'em." I can't help but smile at my son's lung power.

"Daaaddd!"

"Holy cow, Bodie!" I holler back. "Mace and I are in the antique camera museum. Come find us."

A few moments later Bodie and the big cat arrive in the doorway of the camera museum. "There you are, Dad, and Hi, Uncle Mace. I finally found you."

"What's up, Bodie, and why are you making such a racket?" I chide.

"What racket?" Bodie asks. "I was just looking for you, is all."

I look at Mace, and he gives me his you-are-so-lucky-smile. I roll my eyes at him.

"Are we gonna practice some more fly casting today?" Bodie asks. "I think I could use some more practice after getting hung up in the trees yesterday."

"Sure, we can do that in a little bit, and you need to get your gear packed because we're leaving for Northern Wisconsin tomorrow morning. Why don't you ask your mom to help make sure you've got everything ready on your list, okay? I need to go over a few things with Mace, and I'll meet you outside in the courtyard in about fifteen minutes, son."

"Okay, c'mon Satchie, let's go find Mom now!" and the two pals go dashing out the door together.

"It's going to be a lot quieter around here with Bodie off at camp this summer," Mace declares.

"Honestly, I'm gonna miss his, uh, youthful enthusiasm."

I smile at Mace and say, "Yeah, I know what you mean. I'm really glad we're gonna fish the Brule for a couple of days before Camp Voyager begins. Eight weeks of camp is a long time, and Maggie and I are gonna feel a little lonely without him around. I'm sure Maggie will want to visit camp during parents' weekend midway through the season."

"He's growing up, Clay," Mace says to me. "Remember how rough Rennie's beginning was when we took him in, and he sure turned out well. Bodie's had a much smoother start in life, and I'm confident he'll do well too. How can he not when he's got you and Maggie guiding him?"

"There's no guarantees in life. You know that as well as anyone, Mace. I just want him to grow up as a bright, positive kid with as few regrets as possible."

"Amen," Mace agrees.

Mace and I walk around our little, world-famous, antique camera museum that's open to the public. Given my travel schedule for work, Mace has taken the lead role as the curator and guide for the museum for several years now. It's given him a whole new interest in the later years of his life, and he loves telling school groups and other visitors about the cameras in our collection and the rich history of photography before the term digital entered our lexicon.

Both Mace and I pause when we come to the gem of our collection which is the famous daguerreotype camera that I purchased with our now deceased friend, Weed Rawlins, ten years ago in Chicago. It was the camera that the inventor of photography, Louis Daguerre, gave to Samuel Morse in 1837 at the dawn of photo age. For Mace and me, owning this camera is a bittersweet thing. It's arguably the rarest camera in the world, given its history and provenance, but we lost Weed to a henchman's bullet during the quest that ensued looking for Morse's trove of Renaissance art.

"You know, Mace, I still get very sad whenever I think about Weed being gone and even sadder when I think that he never got to know Bodie."

"I know, Clay, losing Weed is a wound to us all that will never fully heal. Not for any of us and especially Tori. Thankfully, we've got Bodie, Maggie, and Rennie to help fill the void."

I nodded my understanding to Mace, and the two of us talked a few minutes more about suggestions that Mace had for the museum. He then shifted the subject to more sobering issues again.

"So, my friend," Mace says, "do you think your days as an avenging vigilante are behind you now that you're an old married guy with a kid?"

"Probably, maybe, but actually, Mace, I'm not a hundred percent sure. I sure pity the s.o.b. who tries to harm our family of friends or who goes after defenseless people," I admit. "It's not a past that I want my son to know about, but …" I just let those words hang in the air.

"I get it," Mace says. "You're a complex dude, and some bad people just flat out deserve what they get. Just be careful and don't get caught. That would really mess with the karma around here. Now having said that, I have something for you to take on your trip."

"What is it?" I ask, and Mace hands me the old Demon camera that he and Weed had fabricated into an electric killing device for me several years ago.

I take the Demon camera in my hand and consider the antique detective-style camera carefully. "You and Weed sure came up with an effective weapon that nobody else would ever recognize as such."

"Pack it with your camera gear for your trip, Clay. You never know when the old Demon can save your ass."

I stow the palm-sized Demon in my pocket and nod my understanding to him. "Thanks, Mace."

"Daaaddd!" we hear Bodie holler again. He's outside in the courtyard waiting for us, along with

Satchmo and Lex. We go outside to join him and to hopefully lower the decibel level of his voice.

"There you are," Bodie says to us. "I'm ready to practice some more casting, Dad. Wanna try it, Uncle Mace? It's hard to do, but I'm getting a little better, aren't I, Dad?"

"You sure are, Bodie!" I say encouragingly.

"Not today, Bodie," Mace says, "but I'll be happy to watch you and your dad if you want. I know you'll do great on the Brule River. I bet those trout will come to fear your name, oh great bodacious one!"

Chapter 4

Hank Splinter walks along the National Mall in front of the Smithsonian's National Museum of American History. The mall is always full of visitors to Washington from all over the world, and Secret Service agent Splinter is relieved to have the protective cover of a throng of people. He walks over to a preselected park bench, sits down, and nervously glances at his watch. The man he is scheduled to meet isn't exactly a friend; in fact he's the exact opposite, a Russian spy.

"Ah, Mr. Splinter," he hears a Slavic-accented voice from behind him say mellifluously, "how good of you to meet with me today."

Splinter continues to stare straight forward as this Russian adversary sits down beside him on the bench.

"What?" the Russian says. "You have no warm words of greeting for me, Hank, how disappointing."

"I'm here, Mikhail, what do you want this time?" Splinter asks impatiently.

"Always so rude you are, Hank, and we have such a friendly history together, no?!" Mikhail Borodin remarks plaintively.

"We're not friends, Mikhail," Hank Splinter hurls back at him. "What is it you want this time?"

"You Americans are always in such a rush. No time for pleasantries. Too bad. I always look forward to our, uh, little conversations."

"Get on with it, Mikhail, I can't be gone too long."

"Okey dokey then," Mikhail exhales. "We have another tiny assignment for you, Agent Splinter."

For the first time since the Russian agent sat down on the bench, Hank looks over at Mikhail and stares directly into his eyes. There is a cold harshness in his expression that unnerves the Russian at first, but knowing that he has the upper hand with this compromised American agent, he regains his composure and discards any semblance of civility.

"I know I need not remind you, Mr. Splinter, that we own you lock, stock, and gonads, and you have no one to blame but yourself. Yes?! Those photos of you performing, how shall I call it? 'Quirky acts' with different women during your visit to Russia last year. Quite pornographic, hmmm? Moscow's women can be very creative … and athletic, yes, Agent Splinter?"

"What do you want, Mikhail?" Hank asks him again.

Mikhail Borodin's tone turns deadly serious. "I want you to keep me informed of where your president's security detail will be at any given time, and I mean every second of every minute of every day. Is that understood, Mr. Splinter? That way we will always know where your so-called leader of the free world is, yes? You have that special encrypted phone that I gave you. I just want you to keep me informed at all times, and to help keep you moti-vated, I have another little satchel for you here con-taining the cash that I promised. You are becoming a rich man, yes? Oh, and in case you're wondering, you are being photographed accepting this money even as we speak, and you were photographed at the other previous meetings that we had as well. You are truly quite photogenic."

Mikhail slides the satchel over by Hank's feet. Without another word, the Russian intelligence officer stands and casually walks away.

Hank Splinter sits stone-still on the mall bench and closes his eyes as if that would block out the horrible situation he finds himself in.

"Twenty years in the Secret Service down the drain," he mutters to himself. "Twenty goddamn years … and now I'm caught accepting bribes from a foreign government … and treason. Here I am agreeing to compromise my fellow agents and the man I have sworn to protect, the President of the United States, all because I couldn't keep my pecker in my pants, and I don't have the character to turn myself in." Hank thinks about committing suicide. Maybe a bullet, maybe a poison pill, but he can't bring himself to do that either.

"Perhaps that cozy dacha by the Black Sea that the Russians promised me could be an acceptable consolation. Shit! Twenty goddamn years down the drain, and now I'm thinking about committing the worst form of treason on President Horvath. Goddamn Russians! What a total clusterfuck I've created!"

Hank Splinter absently looks at his watch and realizes that he needs to report back to the White House. He briefly considers just leaving the satchel filled with money, but he figures in for a penny, in for a pound. He grabs the satchel's handles, dramatically flips the bird to any hidden Russian photographer taking his picture and slowly walks away.

Two days later Hank Splinter and his five-man team of Secret Service agents arrive by helicopter at the Cedar Island compound on the Bois Brule River in Northern Wisconsin. Banks has been alerted about their arrival by President Horvath's assistant, Roxanne.

"My name's Banks," he says to Hank Splinter as he exits the helicopter with his team of agents. "Welcome to Cedar Island, gentlemen, we have your quarters prepared for you in the guest cabin."

"Thank you, Mr. Banks," Hank Splinter replies as the two men shake hands. "I realize our presence is going to be somewhat disruptive to your routine, but we've got a job to do, and it'll only be for a few days."

"Oorah that, Agent Splinter, and like I said, my name's Banks, no mister in front of it. Just Banks, and I understand your mission. Why don't you and your men get settled in, then come find me inside the main lodge, and I'll go over the lay of the land with you. Cedar Island is a private compound, but the Brule River runs right through the Brule River State Forest, and sometimes we have unexpected visitors. It's usually pretty quiet around here though, and that's the way I like it."

"Copy that, Banks," Splinter replies. "I'll see you in a few."

Splinter follows his men into the guest cabin, and they stow their gear.

"Why don't you men catch a few winks before dinner. I'll be up at the main lodge with this Banks guy, and after he briefs me on the buildings and geography around here, I'll give you your specific assignments."

Splinter leaves his men, but instead of going directly to meet Banks in the lodge, he steps into the bushes behind the guest cabin and places a call on his recently-acquired encrypted phone.

Mikhail Borodin answers his phone on the second ring. "Ah, Agent Splinter, so nice of you to call, and how is your day going today?"

"Cut the crap, Mikhail, I'm calling you like you instructed," Splinter remarks.

"My goodness, Agent Splinter, you are always so rude to me, but I do appreciate your, hmmm what is English word? Ah yes, compliance! Thank you for your compliance. You American agents are so well-trained to take orders, yes? So, my friend, where are you now?"

"I'm not your friend, Mikhail!" Splinter snaps back at the Russian in a pathetic attempt to regain some dignity despite his treason.

"We are in Northern Wisconsin in a secluded place called Cedar Island along the Brule River."

"Ah, that sounds lovely, Agent Splinter, and what brings you to this place called Cedar Island along the Brule River?"

"President Horvath has decided to take a brief fishing vacation up here, and my team has arrived a couple of days early to arrange security," Splinter replies.

"How nice!" Mikhail responds pleasantly. "If only our fearless leader, Mr. Badunov, had so much free time on his hands, but alas ..." Mikhail says sarcastically. "Now then, Agent Splinter, as we discussed I want you to keep me informed of President Horvath's activities and don't be surprised if you see other fishermen up there in this place called Brule River. Fishing is such a relaxing pastime, yes?!"

The two adversaries speak for only a moment longer and then hang up. From inside the main lodge, Banks notices Agent Splinter curiously appear from the bushes and walk in his direction.

"Hmm, wonder what he was doing," Banks murmurs to himself. "Nothing out there but the river, critters, and the forest. Maybe recon, maybe peeing. Maybe I spent too many years in the marines securing a perimeter."

Chapter 5

"Hey Bodie," I whisper to my son as I gently touch his shoulder. "It's time to get up. Today's the day."

Bodie yawns and rubs his eyes. "I'm ready, Dad. I gotta go to the bathroom and wash up, and then I'll be ready to go, okay?"

"Well, let's get some breakfast first and say goodbye to everyone. Your mom and Tori already have breakfast cooking, and Mace is helping stow our gear in the Tacoma. Even Satchmo and Lex are in the kitchen waiting for you. You're the last one up."

Bodie pushes his blanket off, swings his feet over the side of his bed and trots off to the bathroom.

Maggie had already laid his clothes out for him, along with a sweet note and a book of stamps so he could write her from camp.

I head downstairs and rejoin everyone, and Mace is already seated at the table with a cup of coffee for me and one for himself.

"Big day!" Mace says to Maggie. "Gonna be a little quiet around here this summer."

"I'm trying not to think about it too much, Mace," Maggie replies, "but I know he's going to have a great time and hopefully make some new friends."

"That he will," I offer as consolation to Maggie. "And, you'll see him for parents' weekend in about a month. He'll be fine, Maggie."

"I know, Clay, it's just that he's never been away from us this long, and well, you know, he's still a little boy."

"Yeah, with the heart of a warrior!" Mace says proudly. "Isn't that right, Satchmo?!" The big cat answers by jumping up on the window sill and swatting at a fly.

A moment later we hear Bodie lumbering down the steps, and he enters the kitchen with a big smile on his face. "G'morning," he says brightly. "Didn't know I'd be the last one up. Thanks for waiting breakfast for me."

Maggie and I look at each other with pride as Bodie gives Tori a big hug and he climbs up on Mace's lap. Lex's tail thumps his greeting on the hardwood floor, and Satchmo rubs his furry flank against Bodie's feet. One big happy family of friends.

"So Bodie, what are you looking forward to most this summer?" Tori asks as she prepares Bodie's plate with eggs, toast, and fruit.

"Uh, I'm not really sure," Bodie replies. "Fishing the Brule with Dad should be a lot of fun, but I'm not sure what Camp Voyager will be like. I mean, I've seen their website a lot which looks pretty cool. I dunno, it all looks like a lot of fun."

"Well, we're all gonna miss you a ton this summer," Mace says. "I talked with Rennie last night, and he wanted me to wish you good luck and to stay out of trouble."

"Do you think you and Tori and Rennie can come up and visit me during parents' weekend too? You're all sorta like my parents, you know."

That brought a tear to Maggie's eye, and Tori reached over and held her hand.

"Hey Bodie," Tori said, "I've got something for you." She reaches in her pocket, and pulls out a navy blue handkerchief. "This belonged to your Uncle Weed," Tori said. "It was his favorite hankie, and I think he would've liked it a lot if you had it now."

"Gee, Aunt Tori, thanks!"

Maggie takes the blue handkerchief, rolls it lengthwise, and ties it loosely around Bodie's neck. "Now, you look like a real woodsman!"

We finish breakfast, and Maggie goes back upstairs with Bodie to make sure he brushes his teeth and looks around to see if he has forgotten anything. Ten minutes later they come downstairs and join all of us outside by my truck.

"All set, Bodie?" I ask.

He nods yes and then goes around giving everyone hugs. I thought Maggie was going to start crying, but she manages to compose herself.

"Now remember those postage stamps I gave you, Bodie. At least one letter every week, sir, remember?!"

"I will, Mom," he promises. Then, he bends down and nuzzles Lex and pats Satchmo's head. "See you guys later, okay?" he says to his pals. "Remember, we stick together."

"Okay Bodie, we're burning daylight," I prompt. "We have a lot of miles to cover today and tomorrow."

We climb into my thirteen-year-old silver Tacoma, wave our final goodbyes, pull out of the brewery complex's courtyard, and begin what is destined to be a trip Bodie and I will never forget.

Some 650 miles to the north in the placid town of Brule, Wisconsin, Marna Philips walks into the cozy cafe that bears her name and greets two older gents who have made a daily routine of having breakfast at Marna's Place. Her daughter, Sarah, opened the doors at 6:00 AM and has everything well in hand in the kitchen.

"You fellas doing all right today?" she asks. "Is Sarah taking good care of you?"

"Yup!" Bertram replies. "We're good, aren't we, Fred?"

"Yup!" comes Fred's refrain. "Happy as a puppy with two peters, we are."

"Right colorful there, Fred. Nice image to start the day with," she lobs back at him. Marna tops off both of their coffee cups and begins to walk into the kitchen to see Sarah when she notices a woman sitting alone in the corner booth.

"G'morning, I didn't see you there at first." she says politely. "I see Sarah got your breakfast for you. Care for a refill on the coffee?"

"Yes, thank you," she replies with a tinge of an accent that Marna can't exactly place.

"I haven't see you here before. Are you visiting for the summer or just passing through? My name's Marna, by the way, and this is my place."

"Hello Marna, my name's Rini, and I'm not sure if I'll be staying for a while or not. I live in Duluth," she replies, "and I saw a real estate posting for a cabin for rent on the Brule River. I saw some photographs that were posted online that looked very inviting. I came to speak with the real estate agent, but the office doesn't open until nine. I saw your cafe's sign and decided to have breakfast while I wait."

"Well, you came to the right place, both for breakfast and to see about renting the cabin. We're a very small community, so not much happens around here without us locals knowing about it."

"Yup!" comes Bertram's unsolicited confirmation.

"If I'm not mistaken," Marna continues, "you're probably talking about the Stine property off State Route 27 near Wildcat Rapids. It's an older cabin and very secluded, so if you're looking for privacy, it's a good choice."

"Thank you," Rini says. "I'll see if the real estate agent has time to show me around."

"Oh, don't worry, Perrin's my other daughter, and if she has a chance to rent or sell a property, she'll make the time for it."

"Yup!" comes Fred's affirmation this time.

Marna rolls her eyes. "They may be old," she whispers, "but obviously their hearing's pretty good. Let me know if we can get anything else for you, okay?"

Fifteen minutes later Rini looks at her watch, takes a final sip of coffee, and walks over to the cash register to pay her bill. Marna meets her there.

"Rini, I just called Perrin to see where she is, and she said she'd meet you at the real estate office in two minutes. Like I said, Brule's a small town, and we all pretty much know everyone else."

In unison Bertram and Fred chime in, "Yup!"

"You've been very helpful, Marna. I appreciate it," Rini replies. "I imagine I'll see you all again if I decide to rent the cabin on the river."

She waves a goodbye to Bertram and Fred, but they're too engrossed in their newspapers to notice.

Chapter 6

BODIE AND I SETTLE IN for the long drive north. "Okay, Mr. Navigator," I say to Bodie. "Have you plotted a course for us to avoid the heavy traffic near Chicago?"

I figure that offering him the navigation responsibilities will give him something to do on a long haul, plus provide him with a feel for the changing landscape as we head north.

Bodie pulls out his iPad and says, "I have, Dad, according to Google Maps if we take I-465 over to I-74 and drive toward Bloomington, Illinois, that'll keep us west of Chicago."

"Then where?" I ask.

"From Bloomington, it looks like we take I-39 north to Madison, Wisconsin," Bodie says.

"Here, let me take a quick look, son, just to make sure." Bodie hands me his iPad, and sure enough he got the directions correct.

"Good going, Bodie, that's the route I would've chosen too. Now, make sure you have our route planned after we leave Madison. It's a long way to Chippewa Falls, so I think we should probably spend the night there."

"I'm on it, Dad." And before too long he identifies the highway routes for us to follow. "My directions say it's about an eight-hour drive to Chippewa Falls, ugh, and then another three hours tomorrow to Brule!"

"I agree, it's a long way, but consider this, Bodie, if the north country were a lot closer to major cities, the land wouldn't be as unspoiled. It's been a while since I've driven to Northern Wisconsin, and I hope to get some good photos along the way if the weather cooperates. I've packed your camera in my gear too if you're interested.

"It'll be fun to see some of the great dairy barns in central Wisconsin, and then after we leave Chippewa Falls tomorrow morning, we should begin to notice a dramatic increase in the number of trees and much less traffic."

The next few hours go by relatively smoothly. We encounter several miles of annoying road construction as we drive past Beloit and Madison and approach the Wisconsin Dells.

"I'm getting hungry, Dad, can we stop soon?" Bodie asks.

I knew he'd be hungry by now, but I really didn't want to contend with the road construction any more than we had, so I'd chosen to drive a little farther than I'd originally planned.

"Yeah, me too, now let's see if we can find a restaurant that's got some healthy food."

"You mean like pizza?!" Bodie asks hopefully.

"Maybe," I say, "but let's see if we can find a place that's got more food selections than just pizza, okay?"

"You mean like calzones?!" Bodie suggests.

"Tell you what, let's see if we can find something a little healthier now, and we can get pizza for dinner in Chippewa Falls. How's that sound?"

"Oh, all right, Dad."

I'm actually very proud of how well Bodie is keeping himself occupied during our long drive. He plays music. He plays games on his iPad. He pulls his camera out of my camera bag and asks some very good questions about various settings. When he pulls my Demon camera out, though, I get very nervous. He's never seen it before.

"What's this thing do?" he asks. "It looks ancient."

Despite kicking myself for not doing a better job of hiding it, I manage to stay low-key in describing it.

"Oh, that's an old detective-style camera that I purchased for our antique camera museum. I meant to ask Mace put it on display but forgot," I fib.

"Does it still work?" Bodie asked.

I hate lying to my son, but I choose to remain oblique. "No, it's really old, from about 1896, and it doesn't function like it used to."

"It's weird looking. Why is it called the Demon?" he inquires.

"Oh, it's just a quirky name that the maker came up with," I reply. "Let me see it a second. I forgot I had it in there."

I'm relieved when Bodie hands it to me, and after briefly telling him a little about its original history as a camera designed to take secretive pictures, I slip it into my jacket pocket. I wonder at what point in his life, if ever, I will feel comfortable telling him about how I've used the now-electrified Demon to even the score for vulnerable people and about my alter ego as an avenging vigilante. Certainly not for a very long time. Hopefully never. I change the subject.

The landscape begins to transition from congested urban settings to more pastoral scenes, and the first of the really stately dairy barns begins to appear.

"Wow!" Bodie gushes. "Look at the size of that barn! It's ginormous!"

"Just wait, Bodie, there's even more to come. There's a reason why Wisconsin is called 'America's Dairyland.' Hey, I brought some music along that I wanted to play for you when we started to see the big barns. It's probably not your kind of music, but it's something that I think works really well with what we're seeing. My dad introduced me to it when I was about your age, although I'm not sure I really appreciated it until I got older."

I insert a CD of Aaron Copland's *Appalachian Spring* into the player and wait to get Bodie's reaction. As the violins opened the composition, I find myself relaxing in my seat even more and watch Bodie rest his head against his window and follow the landscape as it scrolls by.

"You're right, Dad, it's not really my kind of music, but it's pretty."

"Keep listening just a little longer, Bodie, and we can switch to something else when you want, okay?"

Before long I see Bodie's eyes close and he falls asleep under the spell of Copland's winsome melodies. Several minutes later I see a billboard for a restaurant I thought we'd both like and take the exit to the town of Tomah. Bodie's still napping when I bring the Tacoma to a stop in a parking lot in a small strip mall.

"Hey Bodie," I softly say to the bodacious one as I turn the engine off. "I changed my mind. Let's get some pizza!"

"Really, Dad?!" he replies as any vestige of sleep quickly evaporates.

I park the truck at the end of the lot, and we walk into the small pizzeria. The aroma of freshly baked foods makes our salivary glands explode in anticipation. We're both starved. Bodie selects the toppings, and I order a side salad for us to share. A few minutes later a pimply-faced kid brings our food to the table, and Bodie and I dive in like ravenous carnivores. I have to admit the pizza tastes great.

As we are about to pay our bill and drive on to Chippewa Falls, the door to the pizzeria flies open, and a teenage girl frantically screams for help. That's when I hear the unmistakable sound of gunfire outside.

"He shot my boyfriend," the terrified girl shrieks. "Please help!"

"Call 911!" I holler to the kid behind the counter. "Tell them we have an active shooting going on!" He didn't need to be told twice. "Bodie, you stay here with the girl and get under the table. I need to see if I can help."

"But Dad!" he protests with fear on his face. "I want to help too."

"Bodie, you can help by staying with this girl and don't come out until I come back for you," I command.

I go to the door and scan the parking lot for the shooter. I hear gunfire explode again and see an elderly man fall to the ground as the shooter enters a nearby auto parts store. Bang, pow. More gunfire erupts. I know I have to do something, but I'm very worried about leaving Bodie behind.

"Stay here, son, and wait for the police! I mean it, Bodie!"

I exit the pizzeria and see the girl's boyfriend lying in a pool of blood. I run over to him to see if I can assist him but see him lying on his back, his legs splayed out in awkward positions, with the vacant stare of death on his open eyes. "Shit!" I curse.

More shots erupt from inside the auto parts store, and I see a guy manage to stagger to its entrance. Another shot rings out, and the man falls in a heap, dead.

I duck down behind a truck and pray the shooter doesn't move on to the pizzeria. "Where are the damn cops?!" I cry out loud.

Bang! Another shout rings out, and I see a young man dressed in jeans wearing a dark hoodie emerge with what looks like a large caliber handgun with an extended clip. He moves quickly across the parking lot toward his old, battered-looking Chevy Camaro.

"Hey asshole!" I scream at him, trying to distract him long enough for the police to arrive. Sirens sound in the distance, but I know this prick has a good chance of escaping unless I can slow him down. My shout at him brings a salvo of gunshots in my direction, and I duck behind the safety of the truck again. I dare a peek over the truck's hood and see the menacing figure get into his car and start the engine. It's then that I feel a familiar shape in my jacket pocket, and I pull out the antique Demon camera.

I hesitate briefly, then run in a crouched posture toward the shooter as he puts his car in gear and begins screeching his tires in an effort to get away. I close the distance to within fifteen feet, and he stares in my direction with a look of angry determination on his face. I press the button on the Demon camera, and a bolt of blue electricity discharges and melts his front left tire, and I see smoke billow from under the hood of his car. The car is finished, but the shooter isn't. He bolts out of the driver's seat just as the first police cruiser speeds into the lot. The cruiser is followed by a second and then a third. They have the shooter surrounded, and I run back to the pizzeria to check on Bodie. He and the girl are okay.

"Hey Bodie, c'mon!" I shout. "I don't want to hang around for this."

He runs over to me, and I drag him out the door and in the opposite direction from the action.

"Let's go!" I command at him again, and we run for our Tacoma. Two more police cruisers speed into the lot, and they have the shooter totally pinned down. Bodie and I dive into our truck, and I spy a rear exit to the lot.

"Don't you want to see what happens?!" Bodie asks me.

"Uh, no, the Tomah cops can take it from here, and I really don't want us to get any more involved. They'll detain us for debriefing for hours, and I don't see what else we can do. I managed to stop the shooter long enough for the police to arrive, but now we're out of here!"

We manage to exit the lot from the rear of the strip mall without the cops seeing us, and I drive our truck onto an adjacent service road. I look into my rearview mirror and see that the police have the shooter on the ground next to his smoking car. The attack is finally over, but the loss of life will likely haunt the families of the victims forever.

I glance over at Bodie and see a look of pained confusion etched on his face. "Why did that man do that? Why did he want to hurt those people?" he beseeches me.

"I don't know, Bodie," comes my frank reply. "I just don't know."

We drive the rest of the way to Chippewa Falls in silence, but I know I'll have to have an adult conversation with my son fairly soon.

Chapter 7

Hank Splinter steps onto the porch of Cedar Island's main lodge, opens the front door, and walks inside. As a vacation destination for a sitting President of the United States, the old wooden structure is modest in its initial appearance, but for a fishing lodge in the middle of nowhere, it's about as warm and inviting a place as one could hope for. Splinter's trained eyes take in the yellowed pine paneling, fine antique chairs mixed with midcentury modern tables, and, of course, wood-carved ducks and trout, old photographs of dignitaries who had visited here, and artwork by famous wildlife artists like Audubon and others. The main floor has an

ambience that shows heritage, age, and backwoods culture. He closes his eyes and shivers at the thought of his betrayal to America.

"May I help you, sir?" comes Cecil John's pleasant question.

"Oh yes," Splinter replies annoyed with himself that someone could get that close to him without his knowing it. "Banks said I should come find him once my men and I got settled in the guest cabin. Is he around?"

"Over here," Banks replies from the shadows of an adjacent sitting room. Again, Splinter is annoyed with himself for not being aware of another person's presence. In his line of work, he knows that lack of awareness could get a president, himself, or a member of his team killed.

"I didn't see you over there, Mr. Banks," he says sheepishly.

"Like I said earlier, Agent Splinter, my name's just Banks, no mister. I trust you and your men find your quarters adequate." He nods his head at Cecil who takes that as his instruction to leave him and Splinter to talk privately.

"Dinner will be served in about thirty minutes," Cecil says to the two men as he exits the room as quietly as he's entered.

"Yeah, the quarters are fine," Splinter acknowledges. "I told my men I'd give them their orders after you and I had a chance to talk. Fine place you've got here, Banks, what can you tell me about Cedar Island and the area around the Brule?"

"A lot of history here. The Chippewa Indians inhabited this region for centuries before white men came and mucked it up by taking out furs and trees and copper and such. Fortunately, it's now a protected river and forest region, popular with fishermen, canoeists, and naturalists."

"I understand the Brule is called the 'river of presidents'. What's that all about?"

Banks comes out of the shadows of the adjacent room and stands a few feet away from the Secret Service agent. The two men eye each other with professional detachment.

"Yeah, that's right. Five presidents have bunked here: Grant, Coolidge, Hoover, Cleveland, and Eisenhower. In 1928 Calvin Coolidge made this compound his summer White House. Them, plus other politicians, prominent businessmen, and celebrities. Like I said, Cedar Island has a lot of history. Have a seat, Agent Splinter, and I'll tell you about the lay of the land."

The two men speak for several minutes about the various security issues. "Cedar Island is private property, but the Brule River is public. The island is small, only about two hundred feet in diameter, but the name Cedar Island designates an area covering both banks of the river for about a mile."

He pulls out a map that shows the estate compound, several out-buildings and a fish hatchery.

"Seems manageable to me," Splinter says. "Looks like there's only a couple of roads and bridges that provide access."

"Yeah," Banks replies, "but the Brule River being open to the public provides more of a security issue."

Splinter nods his understanding. "I think my men and I can handle it though."

"I'm counting on it, Agent Splinter," Banks says.

"So, what's your background, Banks? Are you military?"

"Former marine. President Horvath and I served together back in the day. We did three tours together in places both of us just as soon forget about. Now, Cecil Johns and I look after this place, and I guide on the river for people who don't annoy me."

As the two men finish their discussion, Cecil reenters the room and nods at Banks to indicate that dinner is almost ready.

"Why don't you go collect your men, Agent Splinter, and meet me in the dining room. We can all talk more over the fine grub Cecil prepares."

"Copy that, Banks. We appreciate your hospitality."

Some seven miles north of Cedar Island Rini Neff knocks on the door of the Northwoods Real Estate office and is warmly greeted by Perrin Philips. It's 9:10 AM, and Perrin has been hustling around the office preparing to meet this prospective client her mother, Marna, called her about.

"Welcome to the bustling metropolis of Brule, Wisconsin," Perrin says to Rini with an outstretched hand. "Come on in and make yourself comfortable. I just started a pot of coffee, or I have tea if you prefer."

"Thank you, Perrin, but your mother and sister have already served me plenty. Perhaps we can talk about this cabin for rent that I saw posted on your office's website. I believe Marna referred to it as the Stine property."

"That's right," Perrin replies.

Like her mother, Perrin notices a hint of an accent that she can't quite identify, but she chooses to talk about the property instead of asking personal questions too quickly.

"From the pictures it looks like a nice old wooden house in the middle of the forest, very secluded," Rini says. "I'm surprised that it's for rent and not for sale."

"Well, it's an attractive property, mainly because of its location on the Brule River, but it needs quite a bit of work. Truth is, it's been on the market for about three years. The owner has had a very high price on it, again mainly because of its location on the Brule, and it hasn't sold. So, the owner has decided to keep it in the family for now and rent it instead of taking a drastically reduced price."

"Is it habitable at this point? I don't need a palace, Perrin, but I need to make sure it's safe to stay in."

"Oh sure," Perrin acknowledges. "It's definitely habitable. I've got the keys here. If you have the time, why don't we drive over and look at it? We can be back in an hour."

"Sounds good," Rini replied. "I have the time, and I should be able to make a decision pretty quickly once I see it."

The two women collect their belongings and climb into Perrin's car. "It's only about ten minutes from here, and it's a pretty drive."

From her office she makes a quick right turn on State Route 27, jogs briefly on County Road B, and continues south on Route 27. Perrin is very pleased that it's a beautiful day. She points out a flock of wild turkeys as they scatter for cover at the approach of her car. Towering white pines line both sides of the highway for as far as the eye can see, and the sky is as bright as a bluebird with nary a cloud.

Rini is quiet during the drive. She takes in the scenery and also concentrates on remembering natural landmarks.

"So, will you be having family join you if you rent the Stine place?" Perrin asks in a friendly but professional voice. She's curious but also wants to break the silence.

"Probably," Rini replies. "I have two brothers who live in different cities, and they're trying to coordinate their work schedules to spend some time with me. First, I need to let them know if we've rented a place."

"Of course," Perrin acknowledges. "If they like the outdoors at all, then this could be a very fun place for them to hike, canoe, and fish."

Rini maintains her quiet demeanor for another mile or so and Perrin steers her car onto a gravel driveway. They are immediately engulfed in a verdant forest of pines and maples. The smell of decaying trees and pine pollen fills their nostrils.

"My goodness!" Rini exhales. "It sure didn't take long for us to leave civilization once we left the highway."

"Yeah," Perrin agrees, "and the closest lodge is about six hundred feet away. The forest is so dense that you can't even see their place from here."

They round a bend in the gravel road, and the Stine cabin immediately appears like a shrouded apparition from a Grimm's fairy tale. They exit the car, and Rini stands in silence looking intently in all directions before finally settling her eyes on the cabin itself. The only sounds they hear are the wind in the pines and the call of a startled crow.

Perrin looks at Rini and says, "C'mon. let's go around to the other side and enter through the large, screened porch. The boathouse and the river are on that side too."

"Oh, I like the feel of the dry pine needles under my feet. Reminds me of the place where I grew up. Far away from here."

Perrin is about to ask where that was, but Rini continues, "I see what you mean about the place needing some work. The roof shingles look ancient with moss, and the porch screens need some attention too."

Perrin unlocks the door, and they enter a huge porch with old wooden furniture and two beds hanging from chains from the ceiling.

"Hmm," Rini intones. "I've never seen beds hanging from chains before."

"It's a popular thing for people to do up here. The warm season's so short that a lot of people like to be as close to nature as possible."

At that, a red squirrel darts in front of them and exits the porch through a knothole in the floor. "I see what you mean about being close to nature," Rini laughs.

They take the next several minutes looking at the dated kitchen and bathrooms. The cabin is furnished, but the furniture is old and faded. Perrin opens some of the bedroom closets, and there appears to be plenty of clean bedding, towels, and cleaning supplies.

"What's this?" Rini asks as she points to a trap-door in the floor.

"Oh that. The owners wanted to have a private place to store valuables when they weren't here. They cover the trapdoor with a carpet most of the time."

"Sounds intriguing. Can we look inside?"

"Sure, I don't see why not. Mr. Stine told me the family has already removed their more treasured possessions. Beyond that, the story is that Mr. Stine's father originally had the space constructed as a bomb shelter back in the early sixties when the threat of nuclear annihilation between the U.S. and Russia was so high. I understand he was a bit eccentric so I guess this isn't too surprising."

Rini listens intently and just nods her head. She makes no verbal reply.

Perrin pulls the handle and opens the door that is flush with the floor. She locates and flips on a light switch which reveals a staircase leading down to a ventilated room measuring about eight feet wide by twelve feet long by eight feet high. It's essentially a vault under the main floor.

"Wow, this is something I wouldn't expect," Rini offers. "Especially in a cabin in the woods. It even has a toilet and sink. Kinda spooky. Is this the basement?"

"No, there's a basement under the kitchen and dining room. It's mostly where the furnace and water heater are located, plus the washer and dryer, of course. C'mon, let's take a look. The stairway is in the kitchen."

They walk around the basement, and Rini seems satisfied with what she sees. The utilities and appliances seem to be reasonably new, and the space is decently finished. Then they do another swing through the rest of the rooms again.

"Well, the place is rough, and I understand why the cabin hasn't sold by now, especially if the owner insists on a high price," Rini remarks.

"You're right. It is a little rough," Perrin admits, "but the roof doesn't leak and the toilets flush. The plumbing seems to be fine, and the furnace works."

They move outdoors again, and Perrin is beginning to wonder if the cabin is too antiquated for her prospective renter. "C'mon, let me show you the boathouse and the view of the river from the dock."

They walk along a pine-needled path and quickly see the Brule River appear down a gentle grade some fifty feet away. An attractive, well-kept boathouse and dock attract them.

"My, my, isn't this pretty?!" Rini exhales. "I think my brothers would enjoy this."

They enter the boathouse, and Perrin points out that use of the two Wenonah canoes is part of the rental agreement.

"In some ways the boathouse seems to be in better condition than the cabin," Rini says.

"Yeah, Mr. Stine finally broke down a couple of years ago and invested in its repair. No sense in having a place on the river if you can't conveniently and safely store your canoes and kayaks."

They walk back outside to the dock, and Perrin points out the Brule's flow. "We're situated just at the north end of Big Lake which is actually the largest lake on the Brule. Just a few hundred yards north of here is Wildcat Rapids which is actually a lot tamer than the name implies. So, what do you think, Rini?"

"It's lovely, Perrin. So, if I were to rent it for the summer, how much would it be?"

"Well considering no one else is competing with you for it, the owner is willing to rent it for $1,500 a month or $5,000 through September. There's a refundable security deposit of course too. We can go over all of the details back at the office if you're interested."

Rini looks at the pristine Brule River and the charming boathouse. She considers the remoteness of the location and casts a final appraising glance at the weathered cabin at the top of the path. She extends her hand to Perrin. "Deal!" she says.

Chapter 8

ODIE AND I CHECK INTO the Big Chief motel in Chippewa Falls, close the curtains in our room, take our shoes off, and plop onto our beds. It's about 7:00 PM, and while both of us are emotionally exhausted from the inexplicable violence in Tomah, neither of us can fall asleep. I look over at my son and see him staring at the ceiling. As his devoted father, my heart is very heavy for him. In my life I've been a party to a lot of violence, including initiating my own as an avenging vigilante, but this is different. I struggle to figure out a way to assuage my son's confusion and pain. I hesitate to turn on the television because I dread seeing the

news accounts of the tragedy we just experienced. Instead, we just lie there for several minutes, each of us trying to regain our equilibrium.

Bodie gets up and goes off to use the bathroom. When he returns, he lies down on my bed and curls up next to me. I place my arm around him and lightly stroke his hair. Within a few minutes we both fall asleep. When we awake an hour later, my arm is still around my son, and he turns to face me.

"I don't think we should tell Mom about the shootings," he says. "At least not right now."

"Oh?" I say. I couldn't agree with him more, but I think his willingness to talk about it is a good thing, and I want to make sure I can channel this life-altering experience in a way that helps rather than haunts him.

"It would just scare her," he adds, "and she'd probably want us to come home."

"You're probably right," I reply. "Do you want to talk about what happened some more?"

"Not right now," Bodie says again. "Maybe later, I guess."

We both sit up in bed, and I ask him what he'd like to do now.

"I dunno, Dad, maybe go for a walk outside before it gets dark."

We look at a wall map in our room and see that the Chippewa River is close by.

"Maybe we can walk along the river, Dad."

"Sounds like a good idea to me, Bodie. Why don't we bring our cameras along?" I suggest.

His mood brightens a bit at that suggestion, and we put our shoes back on and grab our camera gear. As we walk through the motel lobby, several guests are huddled around the television watching accounts of the Tomah shootings. Neither of us has any interest in reliving the deadly events, so Bodie and I exit the motel and are greeted by the soothing evening air. We climb into the Tacoma and drive about two miles to a park entrance along the Chippewa River. The sun is starting to descend in the western sky, but in mid-June it still provides plenty of daylight for photographs.

The Chippewa River is a pretty stream, not unlike the White River near our home. We walk off the path to the river's bank, and Bodie skips a couple of flat rocks off the water's surface. A duck suddenly takes flight and flies low over the river and around a bend. I can't help but think about the contrast between the deaths we witnessed earlier in a town created by humans and the endearing creatures living in nature. Bodie and I sit on a fallen log and take in the beauty of the scene. He snaps a couple of photos of a belted kingfisher and a blue heron. The heron seems oblivious to our presence, but the kingfisher creates a helluva racket for invading his realm. We look at each other and smile for the first time since we left Tomah.

A moment later the beauty of the river is interrupted by the jarring sound of my phone ringing, but it's okay because it's Maggie calling.

"Hey there, Darlin'," I answer brightly. "We were going to call you later this evening. The 'bodacious one' and I are hiking along the Chippewa River near Chippewa Falls."

I put my phone on speaker, and Bodie hollers, "Hi Mom! How're you doing?!"

"I'm fine, Bodie, but I sure miss you. How's the drive been?"

I'm relieved when Bodie keeps his word about not saying anything to her about the shooting, but he throws me under the bus when he tells her that we had pizza for a late lunch.

"Oh really," she replies. "Clay, I thought you said you were going to try to eat healthy food during your trip."

Bodie looks at me with an impish smile and silently mouths the word "sorry" to me.

"Er, uh, well," are the only utterances I manage to say.

"It was my fault, Mom," Bodie replies in my defense. "Dad looked real hard for a whole foods, vegan restaurant, but we couldn't find one," he fibbed. I gave him an enthusiastic thumbs-up for saving my butt with Maggie.

"Did you see anything exciting on the drive?" Maggie asks.

"Mom, you wouldn't believe the size of the barns they've got up here in Wisconsin. They're ginormous!"

"Cool, and right now you and your dad are getting some exercise walking along the Chippewa River wherever that is, right?"

"Yeah, it's really pretty, and Dad and I are taking some pictures of birds."

"Well, it sure sounds like you Arnold fellas are having a fun, safe time. I won't keep you now, but you can call me later if you'd like, guys. Just remember there's an hour time difference between Wisconsin and Indiana, okay?"

"Okay, Mom! We will."

"And you, Clay Arnold!" Maggie directs. "I'm sure you'd agree that you two have had enough junk food for a while, right?!"

"Of course, Darling, it's only nuts and berries for us woodland creatures, right Bodie?!"

"Yum! Nuts and berries are my favorite!" he fibs again, and he gives me a conspiratorial grin. A few moments later we end our call with Maggie, and we bipedal woodland creatures continue our walk down the path along the Chippewa River.

The next morning breaks with a sunrise that is stunning with its rose and pale orange hues. Bodie is still asleep in his bed, and I quietly organize our belongings for departure after breakfast. In particular, I locate the Demon camera and hide it in my camera pack.

The Demon camera has been my weapon of choice over many years now. My dear late friend, Weed, and Mace managed to create an effective, clandestine killing device for me when I was in full avenging vigilante mode, but it's seen very little use ever since Maggie and I got married and brought Bodie into the world. Love conquers all, I guess, but I've learned that violent episodes like the one that occurred in Tomah can happen very unexpectantly, and I prefer to have some protection. Maggie and I are not huge fans of guns, and the thought of having any firearms around that a youngster might find is not something we want to risk. So, having the Demon camera in my possession is a compromise I can live with.

"Hey Bodie," I whisper to the bodacious one, "it's time to get up."

He opens one eye and looks past me to the window. "Dad, it's not even daylight yet. Just fifteen more minutes, please."

I tickle his foot and say, "Okay, fifteen more minutes. I'm going to make a cup of coffee, shower, and then we should get some breakfast and hit the road."

Bodie pulls the covers over his head, and I go to the bathroom to shave and shower. When I get out of the shower, Bodie is already dressed and staring out of the window.

"How'd you sleep last night?" I ask.

"Oh, so so," he replies. "I had a scary dream about people hurting other people."

"Yeah, me too, but we're together and safe now," I console. "We stick together, you and me, right kiddo?"

"Right," he replies, "but I still don't understand why that man wanted to hurt those people, Dad."

I stand next to him by the window and place my hand on his shoulder. "I don't understand either, Bodie. There are a lot of angry people out in the world, son, some of whom may have good reasons to be angry, but they're some people out there that just have a few screws loose, and they take their anger and frustration out on others. It's not right, and it's not fair, but unfortunately it's just the way it is sometimes."

He looks at me and asks, "Well, what can we do about it, Dad?"

"Great question, Bodie, and I wish I had a great answer for you. One thing's for sure, you never need to let people push you around. As your dad, I want you to rely on your better angels, but I also want you to be vigilant and defend yourself and others in need."

He nods his understanding, but he's also only nine years old. I wish I could always be there to protect him, but I know that's not going to be possible. He leans against me and asks, "Besides yesterday, have you ever had to defend yourself or other people?"

I look him squarely in the eye and answer, "Yes. Yes, son, I have, but I prefer not to go into details with you right now," I answer honestly. "We can talk about it again at some point, Bodie, just not right now, okay? How about we get some breakfast instead and think about how much fun we're going to have when we get up to Camp Voyager and the Brule River?"

I can't blame Bodie for giving me a confused expression. I imagine he must be conjuring up all kinds of images and questions. Fortunately for me, he accepts my suggestion for now, and I wonder when, if ever, I'll come totally clean with my son about my history as an avenging vigilante.

––––––––

After breakfast we load our gear in the Tacoma and bid adieu to the lower portion of Wisconsin.

I steer the Tacoma onto U.S. Route 53 which leads to Superior, Duluth, and beyond. Bodie has our itinerary clearly identified on his iPad, and we leave Chippewa Falls in our rearview mirror.

"Looks like we continue north on Route 53 for about two hours and then head east on County Road P. Our exit is about thirty miles south of Superior, and then we head over toward Lake Nebagamon," Bodie reports. "Then, from there we should only be about fifteen miles away from Lake Winneboujou. Total driving time looks like less than three hours."

With each highway mile that passes, I find myself relaxing more and more. Bodie is listening to some of his music with his ear buds and watching the land scroll by.

"Wow, Dad, you're right, once we got past Chippewa Falls the scenery sure changed. Very few big dairy barns and a lot less traffic!"

We drive on for another couple of hours taking in the sublime beauty of Northern Wisconsin.

"How about the trees, Bodie? Do you notice any differences?"

He stares at the vast arboreal forests looming on both sides of the highway. "Yeah, Dad, there's a ton of them. Looks like they're mostly pines and maples with a lot of white birches too."

I reach over and give my son's shoulder a gentle squeeze of appreciation. I see road signs for the names of towns that I once knew but had forgotten about: Minong, Gordon, Solon Springs, Bennett.

"Soon," I say. "We're getting closer, Bodie!"

"There, Dad!" my young navigator directs. "Take that exit for Lake Nebagamon. We are getting really close now," he says with excitement growing.

We take the exit and turn east on County Road P. Five miles later we enter the charming village of Lake Nebagamon, Wisconsin.

"I remember this town," I say to Bodie. "There's another boys' summer camp on the lake called Camp Nebagamon. It's a rival camp to our Camp Voyager. I remember we used to have swim meets and lumberjack contests against those kids. Good times!"

In the blink of an eye, we're through the village and again driving beneath a canopy of conifers. Before long I see a road sign indicating the Brule River, and I slow the Tacoma down so we can both get a good look.

"Here's what we'll be canoeing and fishing the next couple of days, Bodie. We won't put in here though. We'll do that at the Stone's Bridge landing."

We drive for another fifteen minutes and arrive at a site that I haven't seen in many years. A large statue of Paul Bunyan greets us at the entrance to Camp Voyager along the shore of Lake Winneboujou five miles west of the town of Brule. We've arrived.

Chapter 9

BODIE AND I SIT STILL for a few moments while I take in the scene before us. It's definitely a deja vu experience for me. I look over at Bodie who has a great smile on his face. It's hard for me to believe that I was his age when I first came to Camp Voyager about thirty-five years ago.

"This was a magical place for me, Bodie. To this day many former campers and counselors consider Camp Voyager to be like hallowed ground."

"Who's the big dude with the ax?" he asks.

"Paul Bunyan," I reply. "That statue was here when I was your age. C'mon, let's get out and see who's around. I'd love to show you around some of my old haunts and share a few memories."

We get out of the truck, and I immediately feel even more deja vu moments. For one, the feel of the sandy soil scattered with pine needles transports me back to my childhood. As does the smell of the air and the sound of the wind through the trees. More than anything though, it's the sights of the campgrounds and the buildings before us that cause a well of emotions to rise within me.

"Let's go up to the big house and see if the director, Bern Lorber, is around."

We amble along the walkway toward the large, white, wooden frame house that serves as the administrative office for camp, plus its library and sitting rooms. It looks exactly as I remember it, right down to the wooden sign in front of the big house that has the word "welcome" written in a dozen different languages. We immediately see a host of young staff counselors bustling around getting things ready for the opening of camp next week.

We open the front door and walk inside. Again, it looks and smells exactly as I remember it, and I hope that Bodie comes away from his camp experiences with as many fond memories as I have.

"May I help you?" a friendly young man says as we enter the small office area.

"Yes," I say, "I'm Clay Arnold and this is my son, Bodie. We've arrived a few days early to visit the area before camp begins, and I wanted to show him around camp a little if that's okay."

"It sure is!" I hear a man's voice say as he emerges from a room behind the main office. "Clay, it's so good to see you again, my friend!" says Bern Lorber warmly, "And this must be Bodie!"

I look at Bern and see a fellow who is in his midforties, balding with a protruding roll of chubbiness around his middle.

"Wait a minute!" I say. "I know Bern Lorber, and you're not him. The Bern Lorber I know is about seventeen years old, skinny with a full head of dark hair!" We give each other a friendly hug and take in the physical changes since our youth.

"Yeah!" Bern says, "and the Clay Arnold I remember isn't a world-famous photographer with a kid of his own."

Bern extends his hand to Bodie and welcomes him to Camp Voyager. "And you, sir," he says enthusiastically to Bodie, "are in for a lot of terrific new adventures this summer. We've got a bunch of great kids that'll be your bunkmates in Little Dipper 1."

"Bern, I know you and the staff are really busy getting things ready for the start of camp. Is it okay if Bodie and I just wander around camp's grounds for a little while. We're going to be staying at the Grey Gables motel in Brule for a couple of days while I introduce Bodie to the wonders of the Brule River."

"Sure," says Bern. "Bobby here will give you some name tags so our staff knows that you're visitors. We're really hustling around here getting things ready, but I'm sure you'll remember the place well enough to find your way around. Bodie, camp looks very much like it did when your dad and I were campers here, but we've added some new things too like our climbing wall."

"Cool!" says Bodie as Bobby hands him his name tag.

"Clay, you guys can visit as long as you like. I'll be all over the place, but if you have any questions, our staff should be able to help if I'm not available."

"Thanks, Bern, I think Bodie and I should be fine on our own. I just want to share this place with him and enjoy some great memories too."

Bodie and I step out onto the big house's front porch and visually scan the camp's grounds.

"Bodie, you may recall from the website that Camp Voyager will have over two hundred boys here this summer. Camp is divided into four villages by age group. The Woodsmen village has the oldest boys, and it's over there near the lake. The Trappers are the next oldest, then the Anglers, and then your village, the Little Dippers. The Little Dippers are the youngest kids in camp, and your cabin is called Little Dipper 1."

"I don't know how I feel about being in with the babies," Bodie says. "Can't I be in the Woodsmen village?" he laments.

"Not for a few years, son. C'mon, let's walk over and check out your cabin. Little Dipper 1 will be your home this summer."

We walk over to the Little Dipper village, and I can't believe how much it's remained the same. A cluster of white wooden frame cabins with green-shingled roofs appears before us.

"I swear it looks the same, Bodie," I say softly. "Same trees, same four-square and box-hockey courts, even the old push shack where the counselors hung out at night." I shake my head in amazement.

I open the screen door to the entrance of Little Dipper 1, and Bodie and I enter its magical little realm. It looks the same. Modest in appearance, the way a boys' cabin should be. There's a single light fixture in the ceiling, with the same pine walls and windows with rope cords for opening and closing. A bank of cubby holes lines one wall for the boys to stow some of their stuff.

"What are these?" Bodie asks as he points to some wooden wall plaques shaped like arrowheads with photos and names attached. Each one has a date.

"You tell me," I say to the 'bodacious one.' I wander over to one in particular and say, "Here Bodie, take a look at this one."

He stands beside me and says, "Seriously, that's you as a Little Dipper?!"

"Yup! Sure is," I reply. "When I was your age. Me and my cabinmates and our counselor, Lars."

"No way!" he laughs. Seeing the wall plaque with my picture on it makes him immediately feel more at home. "I can't believe I'll be in the same cabin as you!"

"Yeah, only about thirty-five years later," I say. "C'mon, you'll be back here soon enough. There are other places I want to show you."

We exit Little Dipper 1 and walk toward the crest of a small slope offering a view of the rest of the camp property.

"What's that building?" Bodie asks as he points.

"Oh that's the Jop," I say with amusement.

"What does that mean?" Bodie asks.

"It's the latrine for the Little Dipper village, you know, the bathroom."

"Why do they call it the Jop?"

I smile at him and say, "Well, the story goes that there was a kid from Joplin, Missouri, who spent an inordinate amount of time in the bathroom here, so the campers and staff started calling it the Jop in his honor, and the nickname just stuck."

"That's weird, but kinda funny," Bodie replies. "The Jop, huh?!"

"The other villages are over there," I point out, "and the craft shop is over here. The rifle range and tennis courts are over there and the dining hall is just over here. The dining hall is the heart of camp where you'll have your meals and hear announcements about different activities. And finally, the waterfront is beyond it … lots of canoes and sailboats and motorboats, plus swimming, fishing, and aquatic nature studies."

"It's big," Bodie says. "Hope I don't get lost."

"You won't," I assuage. "Plus the older kids are usually happy to help the younger boys. You'll fit in really well, son."

Bodie and I wander around camp's grounds for about another hour, and I regale him with stories from my youth. I still can't believe I'm back at Camp Voyager, and now with a Little Dipper of my own.

"Seen enough for now?" I ask him.

"I think so," Bodie says. "I'm getting hungry, Dad."

We return to the big house to say goodbye to Bern Lorber, but he's off somewhere else looking after things. I take another wistful glance at camp from the front porch and can't help but wish I were a young boy again beginning adventures with buddies in the north woods. I'm thrilled for Bodie and frankly relieved that we're talking about camp instead of the raw human tragedy that we experienced in the strip mall in Tomah.

We leave Camp Voyager and drive the few miles along County Road B to Route 27 and pull into the parking lot of the Grey Gables motel in Brule. Maggie had made our reservations for us a couple of weeks earlier, and everything was in order for our arrival, including the rental and transport services for our canoes for the Brule. We check into our clean, comfortable room and stow our gear.

"I'm so hungry I could eat a moose!" I say to Bodie. "You've gotta be starved too, huh?!"

"Make that two mooses! Or is it mice?!" Bode laughs.

We return to the lobby, and I ask the desk clerk who's a sturdy-looking, middle-aged woman named Tillie for a place where two hungry guys can get a healthy meal.

"Really only one restaurant in Brule if you're after healthy food," Tillie advises, "and that's Marna's Place just down the road."

"Or, we can just split a moose for lunch," I tease Bodie.

He rolls his eyes and calls me a nut. "No way, Dad, I want my own moose, thank you very much!" he lobs back at me.

Poor Tillie doesn't know what to think and simply walks away.

Chapter 10

BANKS STANDS ON THE porch of Cedar Island's main lodge and appraises the scene before him. It's about 6:00 AM and a shroud of fog looms over the river like a protective blanket. With each moment that passes, the rising sun warms the fog and it begins to slowly spill over the Brule's banks and spectrally spread over the land.

"Perfect!" Banks says. He puts on his waders and vest, reaches for his fly rod, and quietly begins walking toward the river. He glances over at the guest cabin and sees two men from Hank Splinter's security detail exit the cabin and go to their assigned

positions by the main road and bridge leading to the estate.

At dinner the night before Banks spoke with Splinter's men about the lay of the land, and he offered his suggestions for the best way to secure the perimeter in advance of President Horvath's arrival. From life's experiences Banks knows that pride often comes before a fall, and he felt unsettled by the way Splinter and his men had disregarded his advice as coming from some older retired guy living in the woods telling them how to do their jobs.

"Don't fret, Banks! We know what we're doing. Don't we fellas?!" Splinter had said. His comment had brought some demeaning laughter from his men, and Banks's advice was comically dismissed.

"Dumbasses!" Banks mutters as he approaches the river's edge. He takes a moment to tie on his favorite Adams dry fly and decides where to make his first cast. The Brule is now fully engulfed in a heavy fog, but from experience he knows where virtually every rock and bush occupy this part of the river. Banks prepares to make his cast toward the opposite shallows when he hears a man's voice from behind a large sycamore about thirty feet from his position. Instinctually, he kneels down further into the fog to listen to the telephone call.

"Some old habits are hard to break," the former marine whispers to himself.

Banks can't hear the phone conversation clearly, but two things are apparent to him: That it's Hank Splinter who is speaking and that his voice sounds bitter. The call ends quickly, and as Splinter begins to move away from the protective cover of the sycamore, he hears Splinter say out loud, "Twenty goddamn years …" That was all Banks hears him utter and then only the sound of the Brule as it drifts by.

Fifteen minutes later Banks emerges from the dissipating fog and walks back to the lodge with a nice, twelve-inch brook trout that he and Cecil will share for their breakfast. As Banks sips from a fresh cup of coffee, Splinter's words stay with him, and a niggling, undefined feeling creeps along his neck. Like he'd said a few minutes earlier, "Some old habits are hard to break."

"What's up?!" Cecil asks him as they sit across the kitchen table from each other. "You look even more preoccupied than usual."

"Not sure," Banks replies, "but something is …"

Two hours later the vibrating sound of whomp, whomp, whomp abruptly materializes over Cedar Island and scatters a flock of crows that are dining on something unidentifiable in the underbrush. Banks and Cecil come out on the porch and watch as rotor wash from the president's helicopter scatters leaves and debris. Hank Splinter also materializes and via radio he directs the pilot to a small helipad. Cedar Island and the "river of presidents" now adds one more chief executive officer to its list of notables.

Once on the ground two armed and very serious-looking guards emerge from the helicopter and visually scan their landing site. Agent Splinter approaches them to confirm that the perimeter is secure and moments later President Jacob Horvath steps from the copter.

From the porch Banks visually appraises his good friend and former comrade-in-arms.

"He still looks fit," Banks says to Cecil Johns. "His hair's a little grayer, but at least he still has it. Washington hasn't sucked the follicles out of him yet."

"Copy that, Banks," Cecil replies. "He looks like he can still hold his own if push comes to shove. I'll be inside if you need me, Banks."

Banks waits patiently on the porch for the president while he speaks with agent Splinter, and then Jake Horvath sees his trusted friend leaning on a porch rail and strides in his direction. There are very few people who Jake Horvath would trust more with his life than Banks because he'd already done so on more than one occasion.

"Brother Banks!" Jake calls out. "You're a sight for sore eyes, my friend!"

Banks meets Jake halfway. "Welcome back, Jake, you've been gone too long."

The two friends give each other a sincere hug of reunion. For old times and for new ones. They stand apart and look at one another, each guy with a grin on his face.

Jake speaks first, "You look strong, Banks. I'd say that living in the woods has been good for you."

"Yeah, it has been good to me. Not much traffic and nobody's telling me what to do. I like that a lot. And you, you look like you're holding up pretty darn well, Jake. It's great to have you back. C'mon inside, and we'll get you settled in, and then we'll catch up. Oh, that fella there is Cecil. He prepares our food, so try not to piss him off."

Cecil and the president exchange waves, and Jake jibes, "Clearly, Cecil, you're the man to know here!"

Cecil leads Jake to his quarters, and a few minutes later the president finds Banks in his study looking out the window to the forest and river beyond.

"I can't believe I'm back at Cedar Island, Banks. No place I'd rather be right now. Thanks for being here for me. I mean it."

Banks looks Jake squarely in the eye and nods his head affirmatively. "You're always welcome here. You know that. We've seen and shared too much in the world to have it otherwise."

Jake Horvath nods his head affirmatively as well.

"So, tell me what you've been up to, Banks. Are you ready to come back to civilization and help me fight for what our people need?"

Banks snorts a cynical laugh and retorts, "Hell no! I've already done my tours of duty. This is your calling, Brother Jake. There's not enough dough or recognition in the world that could drag me off this river."

"I thought that'd be your answer, Banks. I can't imagine why you'd want to switch this pristine river for a swamp. I still feel the need to be in office though. Too much at stake not to try and do some lasting good, but I swear I do envy you and your lifestyle, and I'm very glad you're happy here."

"I am, Jake, and I'm more hopeful about the direction of our country now that you're running the show."

Just then, Cecil quietly materializes in the den's doorway and properly announces, "Gentlemen, lunch is served."

Banks winks at Cecil for his polite etiquette and says to Jake, "It's up to us to hunt and catch dinner. We can talk strategy over lunch."

Chapter 11

RINI STEERS HER RENTED Highlander out of the parking lot of the grocery store in the village of Lake Nebagamon and heads east on County Road B. She's just gassed up her car and stocked up on several days' worth of food and supplies. She needs a lot of food because she's about to have company. Rini left Perrin in the real estate office about an hour earlier and had secured the keys to the river cabin after paying the security deposit plus one month's rent.

She's eager to get settled in the cabin and prepare for her two visitors. The men aren't really her brothers as she had told Perrin. They are men that

she has worked with before though. Men who are stone-cold henchmen who know how to take orders even from a woman. Now, according to her handlers in Moscow she and her team have the opportunity of a lifetime: to abduct the President of the United States and secretly deliver him to Russia.

Even in late morning the road is relatively free of traffic. No cars in front of her and none in her rearview mirror. She turns south on Highway 27 and drives a few miles until she sees the gravel driveway leading to the cabin. She turns in and within just a few feet her SUV is enveloped in the surrounding forest. She pulls her car up to the cabin, gets out, and listens for anything unusual. She's only met with the sound of the wind in the pines and her own breathing. It takes Rini a few minutes to bring her food and supplies inside, and then she picks up her encrypted phone.

"Yes?" comes a Slavic-accented voice on the other end.

"I'm ready for you," she says. "You've got the GPS coordinates. Bring the outdoor gear we discussed." They disconnect, and she waits for Viktor Ivanov and Alexei Pulasky to arrive.

Rini Neff, or Irina Nefsky, as she is known in mother Russia, then places a call to Mikhail Borodin. "They're on their way and should be here within the hour. Is the ship ready in the Superior harbor?" she asks her stateside handler.

"Excellent, Rini. Yes, the trawler is ready, and your team must be as well … at a moment's notice. You know where this place is called Cedar Island on the Brule River, yes? My inside contact will alert me when it is time to act. Do not fail us, Rini, and great glory will be yours." They hang up, and she waits anxiously.

Bodie and I arrive at Marna's Place, and the first thing we see when we get out of the car are Moose antlers hanging over the doorway. I point to the antlers and say, "Yum!" to Bodie. He rolls his eyes at me again, and we enter the diner.

Over the years I've traveled the world on scores of photographic assignments and have been fortunate enough to eat at some of the finest restaurants anywhere. To me, though, there is nothing I enjoy more than good diner food. I know that sounds rather plebeian, but that's how I feel.

An attractive, middle-aged woman welcomes us as Bodie and I enter, and she directs us to a booth. "Good afternoon, gentlemen, I'm Marna, and this is my place. Please make yourself comfortable, and we'll take your order in a minute, okay?"

Bodie looks at me and without any equivocation in his voice he says, "Dad, don't you dare ask them if they have any moose!"

"What?! Me?!" I reply looking wounded. I swear my son's comment reminds me of what Maggie would say too. "Not even mooseburgers?!" I plead.

He points his index finger at me and laughs, "Don't start, Dad!"

We look at the menu and both decide that a breakfast meal would be great despite the fact that it's midafternoon. Marna returns a few moments later and asks, "Do you gents know what you want?"

Bodie says, "We'd both like lumberjack omelets, and we'll split an order of hash browns, and Dad'll have coffee, and I'd like some orange juice please."

"Coming right up!" Marna declares and heads off to the kitchen to give our order to Sarah.

"So, what do you think of Northern Wisconsin so far, Bodie?" I ask.

"I like it a lot, Dad, and I'm really glad we stopped at Camp Voyager. This is going to be an awesome summer."

"Just wait until we get on the Brule River tomorrow, Bodie. I can't wait to see you catch your first trout."

A couple of minutes pass, and Marna returns with a pretty young woman who Marna introduces as her daughter, Sarah. She cradles a book in her arms.

"You're Clay Arnold, the photographer, aren't you?" Sarah asks with excitement.

Bodie looks at me with surprise. "Yes, I'm Clay," I reply. "How did you know?"

Sarah places a familiar photo book on the table in front of us and flips it over to the rear cover. A portrait with my smiling face beams back at us.

"Oh yeah!" I evoke. "You've got a copy of *Along the Way*. I'm honored."

"I'm a huge fan of your photography, Mr. Arnold. I love your work. It's had a great influence on my own photography. Would you mind inscribing my copy for me please?"

I glance at Bodie with a self-satisfied grin that implies, "See, your dad's not such a moose-munching nut after all."

"Of course, Sarah, it would be my pleasure." I write a warm inscription for her, and she scurries off to finish cooking our omelets.

Marna tops off my coffee cup and thanks me for being nice to her daughter. "So, are you fellas up here on vacation or on a photographic assignment?" she asks.

Bodie speaks up proudly, "Dad's brought me up here to go to Camp Voyager on Lake Winneboujou for the summer, but first we're going to fish the Brule for a couple of days."

"Ah, Camp Voyager and the Brule River! Great places! You're going to have a memorable summer, young fella. How did you decide to come to summer camp in Northern Wisconsin?"

Bodie speaks up again, "Dad went to Camp Voyager a really long time ago when he was young, and we just visited there, so yeah, it looks pretty cool."

I ask Marna how well she knows the area, and she relies, "Well, I didn't grow up here as a kid. Our family moved up here when I was about twelve. We actually lived in Superior, and my dad worked for the U.S. Forest Service. Once my folks got to know the area outside of Superior and Duluth, they fell in love with the Brule River Forest, and well, I've been here ever since. That's over thirty years now. Thing is this land and the rivers around here get in your blood. Winters can be a major pain, but there's nowhere else I'd rather be."

"Do you like to canoe the Brule?" Bodie asks.

"Canoes or kayaks, makes no difference to me as long as I can get on that river and reconnect with its spirit at least a couple of times a summer. Yeah, Bodie, I like to canoe the Brule. You will too."

"How's the fishing?" He continues. "Are there some big trout in there still?"

"Well, that depends on what you call big, right? How about that guy?" she says pointing to the wall by the cash register. There's a twenty-two-inch brown trout mounted on a wooden placard.

"Whoa! You caught that fish?!" Bodie bellows. "It's ginormous!"

"Yessir, Bodie, I caught it last autumn between Wildcat Rapids and Lucius Lake shortly after the first frost. So, you'll probably agree that the fishing's pretty darn good still."

Marna leaves us to our omelets and goes off to take care of other customers. I sip my coffee and look around the friendly confines of Marna's Place. I can't help but think about our Stella's Diner back home in Indiana. I have a feeling that Stella and Marna are cut from the same fine cloth. Bodie and I finish our late lunch, and we meet Marna at the cash register. Sarah shouts, "Thank you, Clay!" from the kitchen and Marna takes our dough.

"You fellas come back and see us now," Marna says warmly, and she slips Bodie and me each a container with a slice of cherry pie.

Bodie and I are both happy as clams. We've got food in our bellies and cherry pie for later, and we met some nice people. I drive across the highway to fill up the Tacoma, and Bodie and I both see two very rough-looking characters at the pump next to us. Bodie and I look at each other. Neither of us like the cut of their jibs. One has dirty blonde hair with a knit cap pulled tight and a big scar that extends from above his left eyebrow to his nose. The other guy has longer darker hair that is held in place by a knit cap too. He has an odd tattoo on his cheek that looks like a prison tat. And they're big. I mean really big and don't appear any too friendly in their big Dodge Ram pickup truck. It dwarfs my Tacoma.

"Bodie, why don't you stay inside the Tacoma while I fill it up, okay?"

He nods his head affirmatively. "They're pretty scary looking, Dad."

"I agree. You just stay here, and we'll be on our way soon."

Thankfully, the two big men finish filling up their truck and prepare to pull away. The dirty blonde driver looks over at Bodie and gives him a simian-like sneer. It's a mean, evil glare that makes my son look away in fear.

I see the evil look directed at Bodie, and my hand instinctually reaches inside my pocket. I feel a familiar shape and silently express my gratitude to wise old Mace for arming me with the Demon camera before we left home.

"C'mon, Bodie, let's head back to the motel and give Mom a call. Then, later tonight I thought we might drive down to Mott's Ravine and see if we can get some good shots of the Milky Way."

"Sounds like a plan, Dad!" he says. Fortunately, Bodie seems to have forgotten about the big scary guys. As for me, I'm happy to have the Demon camera and a kid that I adore.

Chapter 12

"ALL RIGHT, JAKE," Banks says, "let's see if you've lost any of your fly-casting skills since becoming president."

The two men stand midstream just above Fall's Rapids in the Brule about two hundred yards down river from the Cedar Island compound. Both men are wearing their waders, and Banks has tied a Green Drake fly onto the president's tippet.

Banks stands to the side as Jake peels off fly line and practices a couple of false casts bringing his line and the Green Drake back and forth above him in the air. He lands his fly in the water near the opposite bank and lets the river drift the fly downstream.

"Not bad, Brother Jake, let's see if you can place it close to that submerged log over there."

Jake draws in some line and gently lifts the fly off the water's surface, gives it a couple of false casts, and deposits it about four feet from the log. He twitches the fly a little and waits to see if he can coax a strike. Nothing.

"See if you can get a little closer to the log with your next cast," Banks instructs, and as the president begins to draw his line in again, a rainbow trout emerges from below and takes the fly. Jake fumbles to control his fly line briefly but manages to regain control.

"Just keep a tight line and play the fish," Banks reminds him. "No need to horse him in. He's not that big. Let him tire a bit and then bring him to you. Remember to keep the line tight. That's it!"

Jake does as he's instructed and within a few moments the ten-inch rainbow is in the water by his shins. He remembers to keep the trout in the water as he removes the Green Drake's hook, admires his handsome catch briefly, and returns him to the safety of the river.

"Thanks for reminding me to keep my cool, Banks. I got so excited that I lost my composure for a second. Plus, I didn't want to look like a total doofus in front of you," he confesses.

"You did great, Jake, and you'll have your old form back in no time. Just remember to manage your line and relax when you have a fish on."

The two old friends spend the next hour or so wading the Brule and catching trout. It's a bluebird day with a bright June sun sending the fish to protective cover once it rises over the treetops.

"God, Banks, I can't tell you how much I appreciate being here hanging with you. This is heaven. I can certainly appreciate why Calvin Coolidge made Cedar Island his summer White House in 1928. Although maybe if he'd spent more time in Washington that summer the stock market crash and the Great Depression wouldn't have begun a year later. Hindsight's twenty-twenty, I guess, and I really don't blame Cool Cal for wanting to get out of Washington."

"Is it worth the turmoil?" Banks asks.

"Yeah, it is," the president replies. "I've still got a lot that I want to accomplish, like assuring affordable healthcare for everyone and finding a way out of this insane student loan debacle, but there are days when I know I'll be perfectly content just to be a citizen again."

A few minutes later Cecil arrives at their location and says, "Mr. President, your office is on the line, sir."

"Well, duty calls, Banks, and I've got a feeling this may take some time. The Russians are doing a lot of insidious cyberattacks against our electoral and banking institutions, and there's no telling where their next attack will be directed."

"I understand, Jake. Like I said earlier, I rest easier knowing that you're running the show. So go keep the Brule River safe for democracy and tell President Badunov and his thugs to go screw themselves!"

Back in our room Bodie and I get ready to phone Maggie to let her know that we've arrived safely, and to hear any news from home.

"Hey Bodie, before we call Mom I want to make sure that we're clear on not telling her anything about our experience in Tomah. I don't ever want to censor the things you say, son, but that's behind us now, and she'd likely freak if she knew the truth. What do you think?"

"Well honestly, Dad, I've tried to put it out of my mind, but it was really scary. People getting shot, and all. I agree. Mom would be upset, but as long as you and I can talk about it if we ever want, I don't need to say anything to her."

Then, the fine young fella that the bodacious one is adds his version of levity to help lighten the mood. "But, in exchange for my silence, I'm going to tell her you wanted us to get mooseburgers."

"Oh no, you thankless child!" I tease Bodie. "You're going to play the infamous 'mooseburger card,' are ya?!!!"

"Take it or leave it, oh famous father!"

"All right, Bodacious One, I know when I'm licked!"

Then we get serious again, and I thank Bodie for his mature understanding. We've got each other's back on this.

"Now, let's call Mom!"

"Hey there, guys!" Maggie says brightly. "I was hoping I'd hear from you wandering woodsmen this evening. Are you guys on speakerphone?"

"We are!" Bodie and I chime in simultaneously. "And we're having a really fun time, Mom. It sure looks a lot different from Indiana, although the Brule and the White River look a little alike."

We spend the next several minutes trading stories about stuff that we did when we got here like visiting Camp Voyager, or what she, Tori, and Mace have been up to. I'm always relieved when everything's fine.

"And Bodie, tell me the truth, have you and your dad been eating healthy food?"

I cringe because I know what's coming? "Well, pretty much, but you know it can be hard to eat your kind of food on the road, Mom."

"I know, darling, but they have these things called grocery stores too, right?"

"And, we've been to the grocery store in Lake Nebagamon and got really good, healthy stuff."

I give Bodie an eager head shake and an energetic thumps-up for laying that suck-up line on his mom.

"We did see mooseburgers for sale …" Bodie begins. I think I'm royally screwed now.

"Mooseburgers, ugh, blaaahh?!?!" says Maggie.

"But Dad said, 'Now Bodie, you know your mother wouldn't approve,'" he fibbed artfully. I gave him my ultraenthusiastic double thumbs-up. My lovely wife, Maggie, however is no pushover, and she knows the bodacious one is tugging her tibia.

"Yes or no, Clay Arnold! Did you and our son eat mooseburgers?"

"No, sweetheart, but it sure makes eating pizza sound a lot better, yeah?!"

Smart woman that she is Maggie changed the subject. "So what's on your agenda for the rest of the evening and tomorrow?"

"Well, we had a late lunch not too long ago, and I suggested to Bodie that we rest up here for a little while, then pack a meal, and drive south about fifteen miles to a place called Mott's Ravine and take some pictures of the Milky Way. It's apparently quite remote with no traffic and very little light pollution."

"Sounds divine. I sure wish I could join you guys. I can't wait to see the pictures you take."

"And I was reading about this place, Mott's Ravine, and it's supposedly got a lot of wildlife, including wolves," Bodie reports.

"Oh swell, Bodie, there's a thought for me to go to bed with, my son and husband being dragged off into the night by a bunch of ravenous beasties!"

"Won't happen, dear!" I assure her. "You know me, safety first!"

"First mooseburgers and now wolves! I think it may be a Pinot Noir night for me tonight."

The three of us chat for a few more minutes, mostly small stuff. Bodie tells her we're going to canoe and fish the Brule tomorrow, and that's about it. We promise to call tomorrow night and ask her to give our love to everyone, including Satchmo and Lex.

Our call ends, and I turn to Bodie and say, "Smooth move on the mooseburgers! I think I'm going to have to keep a closer eye on you. You bend the truth too well. Now, let's get a little rest before we head south to Mott's Ravine."

Chapter 13

AN HOUR LATER I WAKE UP feeling refreshed and see the bodacious one comfortably curled up in a ball on his bed. He looks so angelic to me, so innocent, and yet I know he sees plenty of unpleasant stuff on the internet. I know Maggie and I can't always protect him, but we've tried our best to train him to be self-reliant and focused when he needs to be. I look at his smooth, soft face and know that he'll be sporting zits and whiskers before too long, and then girls and driving. Man, time is moving on.

"Hey, Bodie," I say. "Time to go look at the stars."

He wakes and yawns and trots off to the bathroom. While he's in there, I begin making our

sandwiches and add some fruit, a big bag of nuts, and bottles of water to our pack. When he comes out, he's wide awake and raring to go.

"What can I do?" he asks.

"Just grab your jacket and camera gear, son. We're ready to go."

We take State Route 27 south about five miles, do a brief jog on County Road B, and then continue south on Route 27. There is no one around. No headlights. Just the silhouettes of pine trees against the still-darkening sky. We drive south a few miles and see signs for some of the grand family lodges that habituate this stretch of the Brule River. Names like Winneboujou Club, Nedodge Wan, Noyes Camp, and Wildcat Lodge.

Before long Bodie sees a sign for Mott's Ravine State Natural Area, and we turn west on a sandy county road leading us into the middle of nowhere surrounded by scrub brush and smaller pines. We slowly proceed about a mile, and out my window I can see the galactic core of the Milky Way stretching vertically in the southern sky with Mars to the left of it. I stop the car in the middle of the sandy road, and we get out. It's incredibly dark, but there are so many stars above us that their distant light still provides a faint glow of illumination to the landscape.

Bodie and I stand next to each other and look straight up. Both of our mouths are open in star-struck wonder.

"This is so awesome, Dad. I never knew there were so many stars."

"And Bodie, consider that all of the stars that we see are in our own Milky Way galaxy, and there are billions of other galaxies beyond ours. Sure is beyond my comprehension, son."

We turn on our red headlamps to provide some illumination for getting our tripods and cameras set up. Bodie points to the sand at the side of the road and exclaims, "Wow, look at these!"

"Paw prints," I say. "Big ones."

Both of us scan the land around us to see if we see any big critters, but we don't.

"Are there bears up here?" Bodie asks with some trepidation.

"Uh probably," I acknowledge, "but I'm sure they have no interest in us … unless we spook their young cubs, or if they're rabid, or really hungry." I quickly pinch Bodie's butt, and he jumps about a foot in the air.

"Don't do that, Dad! You scared the mooseburg-ers out of me!"

We both have a good laugh and then turn our attention back to our photography. I place Bodie's tripod next to mine and help him understand the camera settings I select. We point our cameras south to get the most of the Milky Way's galactic core.

"Let's try an exposure of 25 seconds at f/2.8 with a white balance of 5000 and an ISO of 4000." A minute later we are rewarded with stunning images of zillions of stars standing silent sentinel over the dark landscape. After pointing our tripods in different directions and getting some exciting images, Bodie suggests that we take a little break and eat our sandwiches. We use the tailgate of the Tacoma as our table.

"What was that?!" Bodie says as he stands still and listens for sounds in the darkness. "I swear I heard something, Dad!"

"Aw c'mon. Bodie, it's just your mind playing tricks on you in the dark."

We both hear a loud grunt and heavy breathing, and I say, "Or not!"

We both turn our headlamps in the direction of the snorts and grunts and see a pair of eyes glowing back at us in the dark from about twenty-five yards away. I make a loud sound against the metal side of the Tacoma and holler, "All right whatever you are. Get out of here!"

We see the glowing eyes grow larger and hear the beast's breathing intensify. Not an ideal situation to be in.

I turn on my large flashlight and see the bear turn away from the light. Again, I bang on the side of the truck and Bodie throws a stick in his direction. We both continue to make a racket, and somehow we get lucky, and the bear loses interest and meanders back into the scrub brush. I bang on the side of the truck again with renewed bravado and holler, "And don't come back!"

"Wow, Dad, you saved us from being eaten!" Bodie says in half-jest. "I was pretty darned scared. It looked like it was twenty-feet tall."

"Twenty-feet tall may be a bit of a stretch, my exaggerating friend, but any bear in the dark is gonna seem really big. It was probably just curious, son, no big deal," I add with feigned confidence in my voice. "Ready to take a few more pics over by those pines? Then we should head back to the motel. We've got a full day on the Brule tomorrow."

"Okay, Dad, as long as the bear doesn't come back," the bodacious one says not very audaciously.

We walk several yards away from our first position and keep our headlamps on to help reposition our tripods and recheck our focus.

"Aaaarooooo!" we hear in the dark in front of us. Bodie and I stand very still. Then we hear another canine howl, but this time it's behind us. "Aaaarooo!" And then we hear a chorus of howls and yelps coming from all directions, and I instinctually reach my hand inside my jacket and feel a familiar shape.

"Uh, Dad!" Bodie says, "Are those coyotes?!"

"Maybe," I offer, "but they're more likely wolves."

"Wolves!" Bodie says. "Maybe we should get back in the truck!"

With my headlamp I scan the terrain around us and see an unnerving collection of glowing eyes all around us only about thirty feet away.

"Uh, we've got company, Bodie. Whatever you do don't run. Let's just slowly move back toward the truck."

We begin to do that when we both hear a menacing growl from some twenty feet away. We look in that direction and see a huge wolf standing between us and the Tacoma. Bodie stands behind me and grabs ahold of my belt to keep from getting separated.

"Just stand very still, Bodie. They'll probably move on after they see that we're not a threat to them."

"What if they're rabid or just plain hungry, Dad?!"

"Just stay calm," I reply with my own calmness rapidly leaving me.

The growl comes again and then other growls come from the dark perimeter around us.

"Nice doggies," I say sounding like a total whimp. "Good doggies."

We hear the alpha male's growl grow a little louder. "I don't think that's working, Dad," Bodie replies. "It's coming closer."

Now, I'm not against defending myself, and I'll do anything to keep my son out of harm's way, but I would really prefer not to hurt an animal, and especially not have Bodie see me doing it. It's just not the way Maggie and I have raised our son, but having the big, toothy critter between us and the truck has definitely aroused my defensive nature. I reach for the Demon camera in my pocket, pull it out, and turn the power on.

"C'mon," I say to Bodie. "Let's just walk slowly toward the truck. It'll probably get out of the way."

We take a few steps, and Bodie says, "I don't think that wolf is going anywhere, Dad, or the other ones either."

Just then one of the wolves behind us comes charging up and viciously grabs hold of Bodie's blue jeans near his ankle.

Bodie let's out a primal shout and instinctively kicks at his attacker pushing it away. The wolf snarls ferociously and tries to regain its hold. I turn to assist my son when I see the alpha male out of the corner of my eye. It begins its charge, and I press the button on the Demon camera. A bolt of azure blue electricity meets the beast in midleap and takes the wolf down into the sand. I immediately see the wolf who attacked Bodie cower and lope away. The others follow as well.

The big wolf lays on his side. He stares wide-eyed, but isn't moving. It's fur is singed and smells like, well, singed fur. Bodie and I walk over to him and see that he's still breathing.

"He'll be okay in a few minutes, Bodie. I had the device set to stun, not kill. C'mon, let's collect our gear and skedaddle! I'd rather not experience a repeat performance." And sure enough, we quickly grab our tripods and move unchallenged back to the truck.

"What did you do, Dad? What is that thing you used?"

"Well, I really wasn't ready to tell you about the Demon camera's special, secret powers until you got a little older. It's a gizmo that Uncle Mace and Weed made for me for self-defense. It's really powerful, and fortunately for our wolf friends I had the setting set to stun rather than a more lethal charge."

"Wow, I'm really glad you have it. Can I try it sometime?"

"Maybe later, Bodie, but not tonight, and I really don't want you using it if I'm not around to show you how. It's not a toy, son. Understand?!"

Bodie nods that he understands, but I know how tempting it is for a kid to try something as unusual as the Demon. We load our gear, turn the truck around, and head back toward our motel in Brule. I look at Bodie, and he has a big grin on his face. All I can think about is the deadly attack we survived in Tomah and now these scary episodes with the bear and wolf pack at Mott's Ravine … and we're only three days into our trip. Surely, the really nasty stuff is behind us …

Chapter 14

THE NEXT MORNING we sleep in a little knowing that we're not scheduled to meet the canoe livery service for our trip down the Brule until 10:00 AM. Bodie gets up and scrambles us some eggs and prepares toast while I pack our lunch and organize our fishing and camera gear.

"Wow, Dad, I can't believe we saw a bear last night and got surrounded by a pack of wolves. How cool is that?! I can't wait to tell my friends back home."

"Uh huh," I replied. "This is another story you may wanna keep from your mom for a little while anyway. Most moms don't like the thought of their

kid getting dragged off by wild animals with sharp teeth."

"Got it, Dad, but it was pretty cool, you have to admit. And that Demon camera. How come you never showed it to me before?"

"On account of because it's very dangerous, and you're a nine-year-old kid, no offense. But listen, if you swear to never even touch it unless I'm around, I'll show it to you."

Bodie sees how serious I am, and he replies, "I promise, Dad."

I go over to my jacket pocket and return with the Demon camera. "Originally I bought this camera and spare parts from another Demon camera for our antique camera museum. This goes back about a dozen years ago, before you were born. The Demon Detective Camera was originally introduced in 1889 and was created to give photographers an opportunity to take candid pictures because they were handling a device that people didn't recognize as a camera."

"Wow, it's all metal and has awesome designs stamped in it. The Demon!!!" he exults.

"Anyway," I continue, "Mace and Weed thought I could use a little clandestine protection when I'm traveling to remote places on photographic assignments. Plus, Mace and Weed really like tinkering with stuff. Weed went to MIT for college and displayed an incredible aptitude for making unique weapons. The military tried to recruit him, but Weed wasn't interested. Music was his true passion. Mace just had a ton of intuition and experience fixing mechanical stuff, and between the two of them, they could obviously do some amazing things. They loved the clever design of the Demon and knew we had some spare parts, so they decided to see if they could modernize it into a very powerful electrical emitter. I'll never forget the first time we tested it. Mace, Weed, and I were down in the subbasement work room, and they set up a paper target on the wall about ten feet away. I stood in front of it and pressed the Demon's shutter release button and this incredible arc of angry blue electricity shot out and totally fried the paper target in a matter of seconds. And honestly, they made it even more powerful over time, so that's why I don't want you handling it without my permission, okay?"

"Very cool, Dad, and yes, I promise to respect what you've said, but I gotta tell you it makes me wonder about what other secrets you have. Have you ever used it one anyone?"

"My kid's growing up too fast," I tell myself. "Everyone's got secrets, Bodie. Even you I imagine, and that's all right. Some secrets are meant to remain guarded though, son. Figuring out which ones to share with you and when to share them comes down to circumstances and timing."

Bodie isn't exactly sure what I mean by circumstances and timing, and I take the opportunity presented by his confusion to change the subject to today's upcoming adventure on the river instead.

"So, I've gotten most of our gear ready to go. We have our waders and fly rods in the Tacoma. Looks like we're going to have a beautiful day on the river. I'll clean up the rest of these dishes while you finish getting washed up, okay?"

Ten minutes later Bodie emerges from the bathroom eager to get on the water. I smile when I see that he's wearing Weed's handkerchief around his neck that Tori had given him. "You're looking like a true voyageur, my man," I say to the bodacious one. "Here let me take your picture, Son."

"Okay, Dad. As long as you don't use the Demon camera!"

We leave the motel and drive about five miles down Highway 27 to County Road B to the Winneboujou canoe landing.

"We'll canoe down to this point later today and pick up the truck. I thought about our canoeing all the way down to the landing at Brule but thought we might do that tomorrow instead. No sense tiring ourselves out on the first day."

A few minutes later we hear a truck and trailer clattering into the landing's lot, and a cheerful looking driver named Gus gets out.

"Are you guys Clay and Bodie?" he asks.

"Yessir!" Bodie replies. "I'm Bodie and this is my dad. Are you going to take us upstream?"

"Sure am, little buddy. You guys are the only ones I'm transporting this morning, so if you pitch your gear in the truck, we can hit the road."

Bodie and I climb in the truck. I get in the back seat to allow Bodie to see the scenery from the front passenger seat. Once settled, Gus steers the truck west on County Road B, and before we reach Lake Nebagamon, he turns south on County Road S.

"In about eight miles or so we'll come to Stone's Bridge landing, and that's where you guys will put in. I sure envy you fellas. Looks like a perfect day to be on the river."

Gus looks in the rearview mirror at me and asks, "Clay, do you think you'll recognize the place where you end your trip when you arrive at the Winneboujou landing this afternoon? Some folks miss it and end up paddling all the way to the town of Brule."

"Yeah, Gus, I think we'll be okay. Plus, I've got my trusty guide sitting up there with you."

We drive down County Road S past places with colorful names like the Gopher Hole bar, the

Norsk Heritage workshop, Minnesuing and Hazel Prairie roads. I watch Bodie staring out the window as Gus's truck and trailer rumble along the rural roads. The sun is warm on his face and illuminates his auburn hair. I wonder if he'll recall his visit up here to Northern Wisconsin with the same fondness as I did when I was his age. I sure hope so.

"Here we are," Gus announces as he pulls the truck to the side of the road. "Stone's Bridge landing, and you're in luck because it appears that nobody else is here right now."

We all climb out of the truck, and Gus and I carry our canoe and paddles to the river's edge. Bodie and I make sure we have our waterproof packs with our lunch and camera gear plus all of our fishing tackle. I slip Gus an additional twenty dollars as a tip, and a minute later he leaves us to the alluring sound of the Brule River and our fertile imaginations as we begin our long-awaited, father-and-son adventure.

About four miles downstream on Cedar Island, Banks and President Horvath step onto the porch of the main lodge. It's about 10:00 AM, and the two friends have had their breakfast and now enjoy the quiet of the Brule River forest with another cup of coffee.

"You look a little tried this morning, Jake, did you sleep okay?" Banks asks.

"Not really, Banks. I was up pretty late with our intelligence people, and it's clear that the Russians are being very creative in how they cyberattack not only our institutions, but many of our allies in Europe as well. I've spoken with Badunov several times about it, most recently a week ago when we met in Helsinki for the global economic conference."

"And what did that former KGB thug say?" Banks asks.

"As you might expect he feigned ignorance while he gave me one of his frosty smiles coupled with his quintessential reptilian stare. I really wanted to choke the prick where he stood."

Just then Agent Splinter walks toward the two men and joins them on the porch.

"Mr. President, I have your security detail in place at key points on the Cedar Island estate. We've got the main roads and bridges covered. What are your plans today so I can make any changes to how we're deployed?"

"Well, Agent Splinter, barring the world going to hell in a handbasket this morning, Banks and I are getting on the river soon to fish for lunker trout. We'll be wading the river close by here. Banks says we won't need a canoe today. Then, we'll see what unfolds next. Do me a favor though and don't go spooking any fish by getting too close to us."

"Copy that, sir, and good luck." Splinter replies and then takes his leave.

When Splinter is out of earshot, Banks asks, "How long has he been in charge of your security detail, Jake?"

"Splinter?" the president responds. "Ever since I took office, Banks, and he served in that capacity for my predecessor as well. Comes very highly recommended, why?"

"Not sure," Banks says, "but my bullshit meter has been on high alert ever since I saw him wandering off into the bushes earlier. Just watch your back, Jake. This isn't Afghanistan or Iraq, but …"

"Don't you think you're being a little paranoid, Banks, I mean we're in the north woods with an expert team of young toughs to cover me."

"Maybe I am being a little overly cautious, but even paranoids can have enemies, Jake."

"Oorah that, Banks, that's why I've got you to help watch the watchers. C'mon pal, let's go chase some trout."

Mikhail Borodin answers his encrypted phone on the second ring and cheerfully says, "Ah, good morning Agent Splinter, how good of you to call."

"Cut the polite crap, Mikhail, I'm checking in."

"And what do you have to report?" Mikhail says without any pleasantry in his voice now.

"The president plans to be on the river fishing this morning with a guide. I've got my men at various key points on the estate, I'll be the one personally covering the president from a reasonable distance."

"Hmmm," Mikhail muses. "Sounds like an opportunity to me. You just keep me informed of any changes on a moment's notice, yes?"

"All right, Mikhail, I'll do as you say, but you better goddamn keep your word about protecting me going forward."

"Oh Agent Splinter, you wound me with your doubting words. Of course, I will be sure you are taken care of, Hank. We Russians always are true to our promises."

The two men disconnect, and Hank Splinter mutters, "Twenty goddamn years in the Secret Service, and here I am plotting against the leader of the free world, a man I've sworn to protect. Twenty damn years … for the Russians of all people."

On his end, Mikhail Borodin mutters to himself as well in Russian. Loosely translated he says, "What a dumb ass!" He then phones Irina Nefsky with instructions.

"Deploy your men, Rini, the president will be on the river with our inside contact as the only guard, well, him and some local fishing guide."

They speak for only a few more moments, and Rini replies, "Yes sir, consider it done. I await any further instructions, Mikhail."

Chapter 15

BODIE AND I LOAD OUR gear into the middle of the canoe, and he puts his life preserver on and climbs into the bow. Once he's settled I push off from the bank and sit down in the stern. We both take our paddles and drift into the middle of the stream. It's a glorious morning. The sky above is blue with a few random clouds, and the water is clear with a distinct tea-colored tint from the spring bogs upstream. Long aquatic grasses sway in the gentle current and provide a verdant texture against the sandy river bottom. Bodie looks over his shoulder at me with a wide smile.

"We're here, Dad, we're actually on the Brule."

Honestly, I feel as excited as my nine-year-old son. It's been many years since I floated this stream, and the thought of being with him here feels like a rite of passage for both of us. One more thing I can scratch off my bucket list.

As we leave Stone's Bridge in our wake, the river is slow and calm, and we're content to lazily drift with the current taking in the subtle beauty that humans of different races have appreciated here for centuries.

"As I recall, Bodie, the river is calm and narrow for the first couple of miles. I suggest we take our time paddling down to McDougal Springs and try some casting from the canoe. There are some spring-fed sloughs that feed into the river along there, and I bet the trout like that freshly oxygenated water."

Bodie nods his head absently. I can tell he's just happy to be on the water and doesn't much care where we begin to fish. Scenic, towering white pines mixed with scrub conifers surround the river. I take my camera and shoot a couple of pictures of Bodie in the bow plying the water with his wooden paddle. He hears my shutter and turns around again to give me another broad grin of contentment.

We arrive at McDougal Springs, and the current is slow enough that I can hold our position midstream which gives Bodie plenty of room to backcast without getting hung up in the trees. He ties a Royal Coachman dry fly on to his tippet like I'd shown him, and he remembers to cast a little upstream so his fly can drift with the river.

"Casting from a canoe is a little tougher than if we were wading, Bodie, just relax and you'll get the hang of it," I prompt encouragingly. After a couple of failed attempts to get into the rhythm of false casting from a sitting position, he finally places his fly near the opposite bank. Nothing happens at first, but then a small brown trout rises to take his fly off the surface and swim for cover. Bodie gets flummoxed by the unexpected strike and the fish manages to spit the hook.

"Dang it!" he mutters. "I had him, Dad, and then he got off!"

"Happens to all of us, Bodie. Remember to manage your line and take in any slack."

He nods his head, but I can see that he's disappointed that he lost his first fish.

"Try casting over there near that big rock," I suggest. "We can come back to that spot again in a minute, okay?"

Again, he nods his head, and he prepares to cast toward the half-submerged boulder when he spots a heron downstream about fifty yards. "Look, Dad, that bird and I are both hunting for trout. I bet he's a better fisherman than me."

"Well, it's not a contest, Bodie, but just for fun let's try not to spook him and see who gets the first fish."

A few moments later the heron darts his head underwater and retrieves a colorful little rainbow. The great bird repositions it in his beak, and slowly flies away following the course of the river.

"Well!" Bodie laughs. "I guess that answers that question, Dad!"

Over the next couple of minutes, Bodie makes a few casts, but without another strike, and I can tell he's getting a little more frustrated. He loses faith in his Royal Coachman fly and ties on a Quill Gordon.

"This is why the sport is called 'fishing' and not 'catching', Bodie, you're doing fine with your casts. Just stick with it a little longer here, and we can move further downstream if we don't have any luck."

Bodie nods his head again and casts his Quill Gordon fly to the first place where he'd hooked the trout earlier. The fly begins to drift in the slow current by the bank and all of a sudden the river boils, and a nice brown trout nearly pulls the rod out of Bodie's unsuspecting hand.

"Whoa!" the bodacious one hollers. "Got one, Dad!"

"You sure do! Just try to keep a tight line and bring him in to you."

I reach for my camera again because I don't want to miss an opportunity to record my son's first-ever Brule River trout. Bodie manages to keep his line taut, and moments later he brings the twelve-inch beauty alongside the canoe. I snap a couple of quick picks as he lifts him half-way out of the water.

"You got him, Bodie, good going, son. Now try to keep him in the water as much as possible while you remove the hook. Be careful you don't snag yourself in the process."

Bodie admires his first catch and uses his forceps from his fishing vest to gently remove the Quill Gordon's hook. One final glance from him and another picture by me, and Bodie safely releases the pretty brown to the river.

"Did you get a picture, Dad?!"

"I sure did, son, and he was a terrific fish!"

"I can't wait to tell Mom and Mace and Tori," he gushes. "Can we email a picture to Rennie too?"

"We sure can! Your first trout with a fly rod! Ready to go after some more?!"

"Heck yeah!"

"Why don't we paddle a little further downstream? There should be good fishing all along the way."

I watch as Bodie takes one final lingering look at the scene around us. It's deeply gratifying for me to see my son wanting to remember this time and place. I suspect that in the years ahead, his recollection of this experience will magnify many fold.

We leave McDougal Springs in our wake, and slowly drift so Bodie can cast as we go. He gets hung up when he tries to cast too quickly, and we have to take a minute to get his fly line untangled. Stuff happens, right?! We continue our drift, and Bodie calls, "Look!" as he points up, and sure enough a bald eagle has joined us on our drift down the river. The great bird soars past us on a steady breeze and then is lost behind a curtain of pines.

"How could you ever get tired of seeing something like that?!" I say out loud.

Bodie makes another cast and lays his fly on the water by a sunken log.

"It may be too shallow there, Bodie," I offer, and just then a really sizable brook trout inhales Bodie's Quill Gordon fly, and the fight is on. Thank goodness Bodie is keeping his composure, but I can't get over how big this fish is, and I'm over-the-top with excitement.

"Hang in there, Bodie, try not to let him get near that log. Keep your line tight and let him wear himself out instead of trying to horse him in."

Bodie manages to control his line even as the trout shows its defiance by leaping into the air. His slow steady retrieve pays off.

"Grab the net, Dad! He's starting to tire," Bodie calls.

I watch him try to control his excitement too, but this is a dandy fish for any angler to catch. It's a challenge for him to bring him in to my outstretched net, but he eventually does it, and I couldn't be happier for him.

"Wow, Dad, look at him!" Bodie says reverently. "Look at all of his colors and how sleek his tiny scales are." He takes his forceps again and carefully removes the mangled Quill Gordon fly.

"Hold him up, Bodie, yeah horizontally!" and I take a couple of pictures that we're both going to enjoy for a long time to come.

"Okay, say goodbye to your new friend, Bodie, and let's get him back in the water."

Bodie places the brookie in the water alongside the canoe. It doesn't move at first, and Bodie gently cradles its belly in his left hand while he gently strokes water over the fish. A few seconds later it flips its tail and dives for the river bottom. Gone! Bodie looks at me with a look of thrilled satisfaction etched on his features.

"That was awesome, son, just an incredible trout, and you did a terrific job landing him! So, are you sorry we're fishing the Brule today?" I tease.

"How big do you think he was, Dad, seriously?!"

"I think he was every bit of twenty inches, Bodie, bigger than any brook trout I ever caught, that's for sure. You have every reason to feel proud, and I have the pictures to prove it! Why don't we paddle down to that grassy area and take a break for lunch? Plus, I really gotta pee!"

Chapter 16

Banks and President Horvath put on their waders and fishing vests, grab their fly rods, and walk across the lawn of the Cedar Island compound toward the Brule. Agent Splinter watches them disappear down the path that leads them to the river's edge. He radios his men to make certain they're in their assigned positions, and afterward he prepares to place another call to Mikhail Borodin.

"One last chance, Splinter," the special agent says out loud to himself. "One last chance to do what's right." He winces at the thought of spending the rest of his life in a federal prison for espionage and plotting against the government of the United

States. He knows he's finished. He winces again when he thinks about his collusion with the damn Russians, hoping that they're true to their word about setting him up comfortably in a dacha on the Black Sea.

"I'm screwed no matter what. Better to spend my days looking at the sea rather than a bunch of criminals in prison garb." He makes a decision and punches in Mikhail's number. The die is cast.

"The president and his guide just left the lodge to fish the river. They should be on the water all morning. Now's the time you've been waiting for, Mikhail, but you better act quickly. You've got one chance at this, and you damn well better be prepared to extract me as well."

"Of course," Mikhail replies casually. "We have a large trawler in the Superior harbor waiting for its, uh, precious cargo. Plenty of room for you too, Hank. Plenty, my friend."

They hang up, and Mikhail Borodin says to himself, "Or what, Agent Splinter, you'll kill me, hmmm?! I don't think so."

Mikhail then calls Irina Nefsky, and says one word, "Now!"

A moment later Irina radios her two men who are waiting in the forest just above the Cedar Island compound. They've hidden their canoe among the trees at river's edge. Viktor Ivanov and Alexei

Pulasky acknowledge Rini's orders to move on the president. They quietly load their gear into the canoe, and then Viktor touches Alexei's forearm and says, "Wait! Listen! Someone comes ..."

Bodie and I find a good landing spot for the canoe along a grassy bank, and the bodacious one climbs out of the canoe and securely ties the bow line around a sapling. I hand him our pack containing our lunch and camera gear. Both of us walk over toward the bushes and manage to pull our waders and shorts down far enough to take a leak. Nothing like a father and son fishing and taking a whiz together to create a bond. Okay, whatever.

Then we sit down on a fallen log and casually munch our sandwiches and watch the river flow by. Bodie ties a fresh Adams fly onto his tippet so he's ready to resume his casting. I look at my son and think about how much he's grown. Like the river, time is moving on. At one point I lie in the grass on my back and look up. The sky is blue with sporadic, white cumulus clouds, and we're under a canopy of river birches. Green leaves, white trees and clouds, and blue skies above, and around us only the hypnotic sound of the Brule. It's all glorious in its subtle beauty, and I feel a pang of guilt for what the Chippewa and other native peoples lost when

Europeans arrived in their lands. Bodie lies down next to me and sees the same scene I do.

"I get it, Dad. Now I know why you wanted us to come up here."

We idly chat for a few minutes about fishing, of course, and his thoughts about our visit to Camp Voyager. We say very little about the Tomah incident but carry on quite a bit about our fending off the bear and the wolves. We tease about what brave and noble woodsmen we are, and after we come back to reality I say, "Ready, son, there's more river to come, and Cedar Island is an easy paddle away."

We check the grassy bank for any food wrappers or stuff we may have overlooked and then reload our gear into the center of the canoe. Bodie unties the bow line, climbs onto his seat, and puts the blade of his paddle in the river. I push off from the bank and swing myself into a sitting position in the stern, and we're off. About a half-mile later we come to a sweeping bend in the river, and I see the handsome Ordway boathouse come into view. It's always been a popular landmark, and I'm glad to see that it's been very well maintained over the years.

"This section of the Brule is called Rainbow Bend," I tell Bodie. "For years it's been a popular spot for anglers to catch steelhead trout in the spring. The steelhead are actually rainbow trout that come up the river from Lake Superior to spawn, hence the name Rainbow Bend."

As we paddle we see the river diverge around a small wooded island in the center with a third channel flowing off to the right. We follow the current down the middle of the channel as it bends to the left, and after the island the river flows to the right. We see lovely cedars overhanging the riverbanks and know that Cedar Island can't be too far away.

About another half-mile later we come to a place where the Brule appears to come to a dead end, and we see a rocky constriction on the right.

"They call this area Mays Rips, Bodie, and it's actually more of a rocky riffle than a rapids, especially later in the summer. Why don't we drift through here and position the canoe in the pool at the end of the rips for you to do some more fishing?"

"Aye Aye, Captain Dad! We're coming for you, Mr. Trout!"

We float along with the current through Mays Rips and spend the next twenty minutes or so letting the breeze direct our canoe around the pool. I seem to notice that the river water appears even clearer here, and occasionally I see a slender fish dart around over a sand-colored, gravelly bottom. I can see that Bodie is feeling a lot more confident with his casting than when we first put in at Stone's Bridge. I pull out my rod, and we take turns casting so as not to tangle each other's line. When we finish working the pool, we've caught and released another brook trout, a rainbow, and two browns.

"Not a bad day, eh Bodie?!" I call out. "This is about as good as it gets, son."

"I'll say! I can't wait to tell my friends, although they'd probably think I'm just exaggerating or bragging, Dad."

"Well, first of all, Bodie, we've got pictures that prove you're not exaggerating, and second of all, if you've done it, it ain't bragging. Ultimately, you and I both know the fish you've caught, and that's good enough as far as I'm concerned."

"Yeah, me too! Thanks, Dad," he replies.

We continue our slow drift downstream, and I say to Bodie, "The river forks around several islands about a third of a mile past Mays Rips. The main buildings of the Cedar Island Estate should appear soon on the left shore. If I recall correctly Cedar Island is the largest of the fishing lodges on the Brule. It also has a couple of cool, wooden footbridges spanning the river. For well over a hundred years this was a popular vacation destination for many famous people."

"Including some presidents, right?!" Bodie chimes in.

"Exactly," I confirm. "Look there, Bodie, we can see the first of several pitches of riffles begin under what I think is called the 'Green Bridge'. The local fishermen call these riffles the 'Hungry Run'."

We continue our slow drift, and unbeknown to us two men dressed as fishermen watch as we glide past their hidden position in the trees. Bodie and I drift another fifty or sixty yards, and we see two anglers casting from Cedar Island's landing. They're the only other fishermen we've seen on the Brule so far today.

"Why don't we pull over here for a couple of minutes and watch these guys fish?" I suggest to Bodie. "We don't want to interfere with their casting, and maybe we can pick up a few tips."

Bodie nods his head in agreement.

The hidden Russian fishermen know they now have to be patient and wait for these newcomers to canoe past the president and his guide. Viktor and Alexei are anxious to proceed, but they both know that if they want to ensure as precise an extraction as possible, they need to bide their time. They also see no sign of their handler's inside contact, the man on the president's security team. No matter. Practice patience; then strike.

Chapter 17

BANKS SUGGESTS THAT Jake wade a few feet into the stream where he has plenty of room to safely cast. "All right, Jake, as you can see you've got two good-sized pools here joined by a shallower, constricted riffle. So, you can easily cast to the pools and toward the structure on the opposite shore. These two pools hold a lot of fish. They're honey holes, and I try not to put too much pressure on the population. So, if you catch more than four here, we'll move further down stream toward Falls Rapids. There's good fishing there too."

"Gotcha, Banks. Good house rules. Which fly did you tie on for me?'

"My secret weapon," Banks says lowly. Then he's silent.

"Well?!" Jake says, "Are you gonna tell me? If you're concerned about secrecy, you do know that I'm Commander-in-Chief of the entire U.S. military. I assure you that your secret weapon is pretty safe with me."

"I don't know," Banks ribs the president. "There's using a fly that's guaranteed to catch trout and then there's national security. Tough choice!"

Banks pulls out his Blue Dun dry fly and says, "This little fella has never failed me. It's like I ring the dinner bell for trout when this little beauty hits the water. Funny thing is I don't have as much success with it in other sections of the Brule, but here it's a pretty safe bet. Have at it, my friend."

"Oh, and by the way," Banks continues. "Speaking of national security have you seen Agent Splinter around? I know you told him to give you plenty of space so he wouldn't spook the fish, but I'm a little surprised he's become sorta invisible."

"Hmm," Jake mused. "He runs a good detail. I see your point though, Banks. Anyway, I'm sure he'll show up. He's probably checking on his men. Right now I want to test your claim about the Blue Dun being all you say it's cracked up to be."

President Horvath steps thigh high into the stream, strips a few feet of line from his reel, executes two false casts to draw more line out, and then lands his friend's secret weapon, the Blue Dun, into the first of the two pools.

From our vantage point in our canoe, Bodie and I watch the two anglers downstream about sixty yards away. One guy watches as the other angler casts to various pools and riffles. His casting motion is relaxed and accurate. It's clear that this man is an experienced outdoorsman. Bodie and I comment back and forth to each other about his casting technique and his selection of places to cast. Both of us are learning from his stream-side display.

We watch the fisherman as he pulls in a nice trout within five minutes. His buddy takes a picture with his cell phone, and they release the trout back in the water. The fisherman walks out of the water, and he and his pal chat and look at the condition of his fly.

"Well, Bodie, while they're talking, let's canoe on down there and see if they're willing to tell us a good place downstream that we might fish."

We push off from shore and let the current guide us down river.

"We've got company, Jake. Looks like a man and a young boy. If they come to us, let me do the talking, okay? No sense letting the whole world know you're up here."

"I trust your call, Banks," President Horvath says as he turns his face away from the approaching canoeists.

As we approach the fishermen, I instruct Bodie to stop paddling, and I angle the blade of our canoe to steer toward their position.

"Good day, gentlemen," I call out as our canoe slides along the shallow gravel. "Hope we're not interrupting you too much. That was a dandy fish you just caught," I said to the fellow who had his back turned to us. He nodded without saying a word.

"This is Cedar Island, right?" Bodie asked. "My dad's told me about how famous people have stayed here over the years."

"Yeah, we've had a few," the man said who had been watching his buddy fish.

"I'm Clay, and this is my son, Bodie. We're up from Indiana, and I haven't fished the Brule in many years. Bodie's going to summer camp up here this year, and we came up early so we could fish the river together. We were wondering if you'd be willing to tell us some good spots further downstream."

"My name's Banks, and it's all pretty good fishing," the guide says. "You know, it's a matter of presentation and good luck."

Bodie glances at the other fisherman who hasn't turned to fully look at us yet. He notices something unique about the man, but he isn't sure what it is.

Banks looks at Bodie and me in the canoe and surprises everyone by saying, "Aren't you Clay Arnold, the photographer?"

Over the years I have received a lot of recognition for my body of diverse photographic work, but I puff my chest out with pride knowing that my son is hearing me being recognized by some woodsman in the middle of nowhere.

"Yeah, that's me, but today I'm mainly a father and fisherman," I reply.

"I've been familiar with your photography for a long time, Clay, and I've admired the breadth and sensitivity of your work. In fact, I think we have at least one of your books in the estate's library. You're welcome to come ashore if you want. I'm the guide and manager of Cedar Island, and I know some good spots for you and Bodie to hunt trout."

"Thanks Mr. Banks, we'd like that," I say.

"Banks. The name's just Banks, no mister needed," the guide responds.

"Thanks Banks," I reply, and Bodie and I step out of the canoe while Banks steadies the canoe for us.

I look over at the other man and ask him what fly he used to catch his trout, and over his shoulder he says, "Banks says it's his secret weapon so you'll have to ask him if I'm allowed to tell you."

Bodie steps to the side a little and catches a better look at the fisherman while I talk with this

Banks fellow a little more. A few moments later, I feel Bodie tug on my sleeve without his saying anything. Another moment later he tugs at my sleeve again, and I look at him wondering why he's being so insistent to get my attention.

"What is it, Bodie?" I ask, surprised by his uncharacteristic silence and interruption.

He looks at me and nods his head in the other man's direction. Bodie leans against me and whispers something I find hard to believe.

Banks breaks into a wide grin and says, "Let me introduce you to my fishing buddy."

The other fellow finally turns to face us, and I recognize the face of the last man on Earth I'd ever expect to meet on a fishing trip in Northern Wisconsin.

"Clay, Bodie, it's a pleasure to meet some fellow fishermen. I'm Jake Horvath." He reaches out and shakes both of our hands.

"See Dad! I told you!" Bodie exclaims triumphantly.

"You sure did, son! Wow, Mr. President, it's an honor to meet you, sir!"

"Well, it's an honor to meet you too, Clay. Like Banks here, I've also been familiar with your photography for a long time. You're a famous man. I remember seeing an exhibition of your night sky images at the Smithsonian a few years back, and they were stunning. Weren't you also the fellow who found Samuel Morse's camera and his treasure trove of renaissance paintings?"

"Yeah! Thank you, President Horvath," I say with pride welling up inside me as my son hears the President of the United States acknowledge my work and the great Morse finds.

"And since we're all fellow fishermen, why don't we dispense with the formal titles for now? Just call me, Jake, all right?!"

Bodie looks at me and then at the president, and says, "Cool! Wait'll we tell Mom!"

That gets a good laugh out of the three adults standing on the shore of Cedar Island's landing. Bodie can't take his eyes off of the leader of the free world. Jake walks over to my son and asks Banks, "Is it all right to tell him about your secret weapon?"

"I don't know, Jake, it won't be a secret weapon if we tell every fisherman who paddles down the Brule," he teases. He pauses a second and says, "Well, maybe, if Bodie here promises not to tell anyone else."

"I swear!" Bodie says. He holds up his hand and extends his little finger. "Pinky swear!"

"Well, fellas!" Jake says, "As long as Bodie is invoking a 'pinky swear', I think we may be able to trust him, Banks. What do you think?"

Banks displays a very thoughtful expression on his face and asks me, "What do you think, Clay? Is Bodie capable of keeping a national secret?"

Bodie looks at me beseechingly, and I join in the teasing by saying, "Uh, I think maybe he can. What do you think, Bodie?"

"Heck yeah, Dad! Plus, I already swore with my pinky finger!"

Jake moves closer to Bodie and kneels down to show him his dry fly. "It's called a Blue Dun, Bodie, and Banks claims it's the best fly on this particular stretch of the Brule."

We talk more among ourselves about fishing mostly and Cedar Island's history as the river of presidents. Both Banks and I beam at Bodie as we see him interact comfortably with President Horvath. Just two bodacious guys talking about stuff.

"Clay, we have some very historic photographs up at the lodge that you may find interesting. I'd be happy to take you up and show you if you're interested."

"That would be great. I imagine you have some images that aren't very well known."

"Jake, if it's okay with Clay, you want to take Bodie out on the river and wade downstream a ways to fish above the Falls Rapids?"

Bodie and Jake look over at me expectantly, and I ask, "Do you have another Blue Dun, Banks?"

The president's guide and close friend smiles and nods affirmatively. "I've got you covered, Bodie. Here you go. Go have fun!"

I watch as Bodie and Jake collect their rods and walk down the shore line in the direction of Falls Rapids. I look over at Banks and say, "Thanks, Banks. We're both very grateful to you. This is an experience neither my son nor I will ever forget. My wife's not going to believe that our son fished with the president."

Banks leads the way to Cedar Island's main lodge. As he walks he looks around wondering what the hell ever happened to Agent Splinter. It's one thing to keep a low profile like the president asked him to do. It's another thing to be totally missing in action.

Upstream about a hundred yards, the two Russians hidden in the trees watch as the four fishermen split up.

"Let's go!" Viktor tells Alexei. "You move along the shoreline through the forest until you are downstream from the president and the boy. Be quick, Alexei! Radio me when you're in a good position, and then I'll canoe to a point above them. We'll have them between us with no one else around."

Chapter 18

Bodie and Jake amble over rocks and small boulders as they move down the west bank of the Brule. They leave the two pools behind them that Banks and Jake fished near Cedar Island's landing and soon come to another pool about a hundred yards down river.

"It's shallow enough here for me to cross the stream. That'll give us enough space so that we can both fish this pool, okay?"

"Sounds good to me, Jake!" Bodie affirms with an air of familiarity.

President Horvath wades across the stream and sees that Bodie already has his fly rod in motion. He

watches Bodie do a couple of false casts to shoot out more line and land his Blue Dun on to the surface of the north side of the pool.

"Nice cast, young fella," Jake says. "So how long have you been a fly fisherman, Bodie?"

"Well, to be honest, sir, today's my first day. At that, a ten-inch brown trout rises to take Bodie's Blue Dun, and a minute later the bodacious one manages to land the fish on his own, without embarrassing himself in front of the President of the United States. He remembers to keep his trout in the water as much as possible as he uses his forceps to remove the Blue Dun's hook. A moment later the trout is released, and Bodie stands and looks across the river at Jake who's giving him an enthusiastic thumbs-up.

The two of them continue to fish the pool, and both of them catch and release a couple of trout each.

"Hey Bodie, why don't we wade a little further downstream? Banks says there's a good pool that holds a lot of fish about fifty yards above the Falls Rapids."

"Yeah! I'm game! This is great!" Bodie exclaims.

For a few minutes they clamber over rocks and tree branches until they come to the pool that Banks had recommended. They take some time to reapply the dry fly dressing on their Blue Duns and visually scan the pool for rising trout.

Alexei Pulasky is out of breath from his jaunt through the trees along the east bank of the Brule River. Despite his youth and training, running through thick woods with waders and a fly rod is an exerting experience for him. Through the trees he sees the president and the young boy arrive at the pool and begin fishing. He calms his breathing and radios Viktor Ivanov who is in their canoe just above Cedar Island.

"I see them, and I'm in position just at the top of the rapids. Canoe toward us now, and when I see you, I will make my move. Then come help!"

Bodie and Jake have taken up casting positions about twenty yards from each other on the west side of the pool. "All right, Bodie," the president calls out, "We're both using Blue Duns. Let's see who catches the first trout here."

"You're on!" the bodacious one hurls back at the leader of the free world.

Both guys select inviting places to cast to. Bodie sees a sunken stump, and Jake eyes a sunken boulder. They use relatively short roll casts so as not to get hung up in the vegetation behind them. Neither fisherman gets a strike for the first five minutes, and then the president shouts out, "Fish on!"

"Cool, but it doesn't count unless you land him, Jake!" Bodie ribs the president. A moment later,

Bodie hollers, "Fish on!" And the two of them are doing their level best to win their little contest.

Jake Horvath has the age, experience, and tenacity over Bodie, all the more reason he's a little chagrined when his trout spits out the Blue Dun just as he's about to net him.

"Shit! Lost him!" Jake bellows in frustration.

"Language, Mr. President! No bad words!" Bodie chides maturely. The bodacious one continues to retrieve his fish when all of a sudden his line goes totally slack. "He broke off!" Bodie screams. "Dang it!"

"Uh, language, Mr. Arnold!" Jake lobs back at him. "But, I'm willing to give you a presidential pardon if you catch the next fish."

"You're on!" Bodie shouts again, and the two fishermen reapply dressing to their dry flies and return to their casting. A few minutes later Bodie hooks a really nice rainbow, and he manages to keep it from diving under an overhanging bush when the crafty fish finds another potential haven. It aims for a sunken log, and Bode walks further into the stream up to his waist to get a better angle. Jake sees that his young friend has a good fish on the line, and he walks down the bank to join Bodie for the grand finale.

"You've got him, Bodie. Just keep your line taut, and I'll use my net."

Sure enough, the two work together and soon net Bodie's sixteen-inch rainbow. "Great fish, young fella! I guess you've earned your presidential pardon," Jake laughs. "Banks's Blue Dun does the trick again, well, that and a darn good angler."

"Thanks!" Bodie beams. "I'm never sure I'll be able to land them once I catch them."

"I know," Jake confirms. "It can definitely be humbling."

Just then Bodie notices another fisherman wading the stream around forty feet away between them and the beginning of Falls Rapids.

"Wonder where he came from," Bodie says as he points the man out to the president.

"Good question," Jake replies, "but the Brule River Forest is public land." From the back of his mind, however, he recalls Banks wondering where the hell Agent Splinter is. Just in case he reaches for his radio to talk with Splinter, and realizes he left it in the lodge.

The newcomer sees Bodie and Jake standing together and offers them a friendly wave as he wades through a shallow run and approaches their position. From about twenty feet away he says, "Nice fish, you catch!" Jake recognizes his accent as sounding a little eastern European. The man keeps coming closer.

"Thanks!" Bodie replies, and then his voice goes silent when he recognizes the man as one of the two creepy-looking men he and his dad saw when they were gassing up the Tacoma in Brule.

The man keeps walking toward them and grins evilly displaying a mouthful of discolored teeth. From behind the president and the boy Alexei sees Viktor quickly paddling their canoe. Jake's training as a marine tells him they are at some level of risk. He sees the fisherman look upriver past him, and he turns to see a canoeist aggressively paddling in their direction.

Jake turns back to face the new fisherman when he receives a vicious chop to his neck that brings him to his knees. He gets up quickly, smarting from the nasty strike and receives another blow to his solar plexus. Bodie instantly screams, "Get off of him!" and charges at the attacker. Jake manages to regain his wind, and he follows Bodie into the fray and delivers a presidential fist to the man's nose. Blood and snot spray as the attacker recoils in pain.

Viktor lands the canoe, and leaps to assist Alexei. He jumps on the president's back, and Bodie tries to grab Viktor's legs. The Russian gives Bodie a painful punch to his side, and Bodie lands in the river shaken. The two Russians attack Jake Horvath, but his marine training kicks in. He manages to land another serious strike to Alexei's face, but the Russian charges him like a wounded animal. Alexei is battered, and Jake pushes him away. He kicks the Russian's feet out from under him and prepares to deliver an incapacitating strike.

"That's enough, Mr. President!" the Russian commands in heavily-accented English. Jake sees Viktor standing over Bodie in the river with a knife to his throat. "I will kill this boy. Yes, it will not be pleasant, but I will kill this boy. Now stand down."

Jake quickly assesses the situation and knows all too well that this man will do as he says. He stands still waiting for another attack. Alexei regains his composure, reaches inside his vest pocket, and approaches the president. Jake instinctively kicks at Alexei's groin, and again the Russian falters.

Viktor grabs Bodie's hair, bearing his throat and draws the blade along his cheek. Jake watches as a small blood-red line forms near Bodie's ear.

"All right," Jake shouts. "That's enough. You're a real big man hurting a boy, aren't you?!"

Alexei staggers forward and takes the object that he had retrieved from his vest and jabs a needle into Jake Horvath's neck. The president swats him away, and Bodie manages to free himself and runs to his aid. The sedative from the needle begins to take effect, and Jake's knees begin to buckle. A moment later he lays unconsciously on the west bank of the Brule River.

Bodie begins to demand, "Why did you do that?!" when he feels a sharp sting to his neck from Viktor's syringe. A moment later he swoons from the effects of the sedative and falls in a heap on the ground next to President Jacob Horvath.

Viktor Ivanov moves quickly. He helps Alexei to his feet, and together the two Russian henchmen duct tape the president and the boy's hands and feet, gag them, and dump them unceremoniously in the middle of the canoe. They cover them with a tarp, collect their fishing tackle, and look around to see if anyone has seen them. The only eyes watching them are those of Agent Hank Splinter peering at them from behind a large white pine several yards away. "Twenty goddamn years …" he mutters to himself.

Agent Splinter leaps out from behind the pine and hollers, "Hey hold on there! You're not taking them anywhere. My men have you surrounded. Now give it up!" Hank lies.

The Russians look around them to spot Splinter's backup. They see no one and call his bluff. Viktor reaches inside his waders, pulls out his silenced Makarov 9mm pistol, and puts a bullet into the hapless agent's chin. Hank Splinter drops lifelessly to the fertile soil. His twenty years with the Secret Service has irreparably come to an end.

"Let's go! Quickly now!" Alexei says to Viktor, and a few moments later their canoe is riding low in the swift current of the Falls Rapids moving further away from the safety of the Cedar Island estate with each second that passes.

Chapter 19

BANKS AND I EXIT THE Cedar Island lodge after he showed me vintage photographs of presidents and celebrities who visited here over the past century and a half. Some of the candid photos of people like Ulysses S. Grant fishing without a shirt are very unique in the archives of presidential memorabilia. I doubt that many of these images have ever been made available for public viewing. Excellent collection.

"I think we better make sure Bodie hasn't gotten the president all wrapped up in his fly line," I advise. "He may be a former marine and the leader of the free world, but I know the bodacious one, and anything can happen."

"He seems like a fine lad, Clay," Banks replies. "Never had any kids of my own, but I certainly know a good kid when I see one."

"He's a pistol, that's for sure. Let's go save the president from his juvenile shenanigans."

We walk the path to the river's edge, and Banks and I see neither Jake nor Bodie.

"They're probably giving their Blue Duns a workout in that pool above the Falls Rapids. Let's head down there and see what they've caught," Banks suggests.

Banks can't stop wondering what the hell happened to Agent Splinter. He tries to radio the agent, but his call goes unanswered. Next, Banks radios Agent Blackburn, the number two man in the president's security detail and is answered right away.

"This is Banks up at the landing. Is Agent Splinter with you?"

"No sir," comes the reply. "We've been trying to reach him also but without success. We assumed he was with you."

"You better get over here, Agent Blackburn. Something tells me we've had a serious security breach. Mr. Arnold and I are heading downstream toward the Falls Rapids. Meet us there."

I sense the genuine concern in Banks's voice and call out, "Bodie! Where are you, son?" My shout is returned only by the sound of wind in the trees and the rhythmic flow of the Brule.

Banks and I clamber over stones and organic debris on the river bank, and from depressions in the moist soil we see where Bodie and Jake were standing when casting to the first two pools.

"Bodie!" I shout loudly, but again there is no audible response.

Banks is moving very quickly, and I struggle to keep up with him along the shore. When we get to a place about fifty yards above the Falls Rapids I nearly run into Banks when he pulls up quickly.

"Shit!" he hollers between clenched teeth. "Dammit to hell!"

It's then that I see the lifeless shape of Agent Splinter laying in a heap at the edge of the forest. We walk over to him and see that he's quite dead. His eyes are open and stare toward the sky. A dark red hole dominates what used to be a strong chin. Just then Agent Blackburn comes running through the woods to meet us and sees his former commander staring vacantly at the sky.

"What the …" he begins. "Where's the president?" he asks with fear rising in his voice.

"You tell me!" Banks says without any attempt to hide his annoyance. "You and your men are the friggin' security detail, Agent Blackburn."

"Bodie!" I shout out again. "Where are you, Bodie?!" No answer.

The agent immediately radios his fellow agents, and informs them that the president is missing and has likely been abducted. Half of the security team maintains watch over the two roads and bridges leading to the compound while the other half collapses its perimeter around the estate. The security officers begin combing every inch of land between them and the river. Agent Blackburn radios the director of the Department of Homeland Security and has the unthinkable task of informing him that the President of the United States is missing and presumably abducted. Then, all hell breaks loose. Phones ring. Radios squawk. People are moving fast.

Banks stands next to me and says, "In about thirty minutes this place is going to begin swarming like a hornet's nest. As remote as we are, the calmness of this place is gonna be gone."

"Fine with me!" I say frankly. "Bring on the troops! I just want my son back safely."

"C'mon!" Banks says. "Let's continue looking some more before a thousand feet start tromping on everything."

We continue to scour the woods on both sides of the Brule, and all along the way I keep shouting out Bodie's name. And then I think, "Oh my God, what am I gonna tell Maggie?!" I continue to call out Bodie's name, and my blood begins to boil with fright and anger. "Bodeee!"

With Alexei in the bow of their canoe, Viktor silently guides them and their unconscious passengers past a couple of large boulders left of center in the Falls Rapids. Alexei is physically battered from his fight with President Horvath, but he's able to call Rini to give her a status report.

"We have caught the big fish and are heading to your position," he says in Russian. "We also have a little minnow too."

Rini is both elated by the great news of the president's abduction and confused by Alexei's minnow reference. "What do you mean by minnow?"

"The president was fishing with a young boy, and we had no choice but to sedate and snatch him as well. No sense leaving him behind so he could tell the American security forces who we are and what occurred."

"Well, what is done is done," Rini replies. "Perhaps we can use the boy as leverage if we need to. You have my coordinates, yes?! How long before you arrive?"

"Soon," Alexei responds. "Perhaps twenty minutes, no more. We are moving quickly through the rapids, but we'll have to paddle hard through the river's lakes leading to your position."

"I will have everything ready for your arrival," Rini confirms. "I'll meet you on the dock. Pull your canoe into the boathouse when you arrive, and then we must move very fast to hide our, uh, guests."

Alexei and Viktor paddle out of the Falls Rapids and soon come to Big Twin Rapids at the south end of Sucker Lake. They navigate past a fallen tree lying across most of the river and then paddle vigorously across the length of Sucker Lake. After the lake the Brule River runs through a narrow constriction with a Class I rapids called the Little Twin Rapids which leads them into Big Lake. They are getting closer to their destination with Rini, but they first need to paddle nearly a mile in open water across Big Lake.

"Paddle hard, Alexei!" Viktor exhorts from the stern. "We do not want to be seen in open water. Put your back into it!"

The two Russian agents paddle as if their lives depend on it across the expanse of Big Lake without seeing any other canoeists along the way. They're getting closer and beginning to feel ebullient for what they've achieved on behalf of Mother Russia.

"Look there," Alexei shouts and points. "The boathouse is just ahead on river right."

Three minutes later they spot Rini standing on the dock near the entrance to her cabin's boathouse. They guide their canoe into the boathouse, and Rini immediately closes the door behind them. She runs inside to see their catch.

"Ah, you have done extremely well!" she praises Viktor and Alexei as they pull the tarp off the still sedated American president and the little minnow. "We must carry them up the path to the cabin and then inside."

Alexei and Viktor are both strong men, but they struggle as they carry Jake Horvath's limp 6'2" 200-pound frame up the path's uneven terrain. Once inside Rini opens the door in the cabin's floor that reveals the old bomb shelter now used for storage. They tumble him down the steps and lean him against a wall. Then while Alexei and Rini watch over their prize, Viktor returns to the boathouse and retrieves Bodie's unconscious body as well. Once the two abductees are safely inside the hidden shelter, she gives them explicit instructions.

"You must remain in here until I say it is safe to come out. Not one sound from anyone. Total silence and no lights, understood?! I will place the carpet over the trapdoor in the floor. With any luck we will be able to evade the Americans who are surely going to search every millimeter of river and forest. If the president and boy regain consciousness, you must sedate them again so they can't give our position away. I will return to the dock and hopefully misdirect anyone who comes looking for them. Do you understand? Our lives depend on it."

The two experienced Russian operatives understand the precariousness of their situation. Snatching the president is one thing. Getting him out of America and back to Russia is an entirely different proposition.

Rini conceals their location below the floor with the large area rug and table and scurries down the path to the dock at river's edge. She uses her encrypted phone to call Mikhail Borodin. "The big fish is in the net. I will keep you informed."

"Excellent, Rini, you have done very well indeed. Let me know the minute you feel it is safe to make the next move in your journey home. Our trawler in the Superior harbor is ready to sail at a moment's notice."

"I shall, Mikhail, but you should know that the Americans have two additional motivations to find us. It was necessary for Alexei and Viktor to abduct a young boy who was with the president, and they had to assassinate your inside contact with the president's security detail."

"Well, we have certainly humiliated the arrogant Americans. The boy is of no consequence to us. Keep him alive until he has no value to us. The president's the only prize I care about. Prepare yourself, though, the Americans will not take kindly to our assault." Mikhail intones. "And alas, poor Agent Splinter, I knew him well."

Rini and Mikhail end their call, and she sits down on a deck chair with a good book. Before long she hears the insistent thrumming of helicopter rotors as they begin their approach to Cedar Island. She knows that a visit from some very serious and heavily armed people is inevitable.

Chapter 20

Banks and I search the Brule downstream to the point where the Falls Rapids begins. After several minutes of fruitless frantic searching, we finally decide to head back to the lodge to help organize the search. When we arrive, Banks's old friend Muggs Larabee, the Douglas County Sheriff, is already waiting for us with three of his officers.

"Hey Muggs," Banks say evenly. "I'm not surprised that you're first on the scene. We think they got the president and Mr. Arnold's son, Bodie."

"Who's they?" Sherrif Larabee asks. "My dispatcher heard a lot of squawking on the radio and thought we better get out here."

"Not sure, yet," Banks replies, "but Jake Horvath was telling me about a whole lot of increased Russian meddling that's been going on. That's where I'd put my money. They're brazen, sneaky, and deadly. We found the leader of the security detail downriver a ways with a bullet in his face."

Just then we hear the sound of multiple tires on the gravel road, coupled with a radio call from Agent Blackburn.

"I tried to stop them at the bridge, but they poured through. Christ in a canoe! We got more coming and now there's three helicopters circling the estate. I look over at Banks and see a frown form on his face.

"Shit!" he says to me. "As if it's not horrible enough that we lost the president and your son, probably to a bunch of nasty Russians, now things are about to get military-macho and real political."

A moment later a first lieutenant with the Wisconsin National Guard bounds out of his car and heads in our direction.

"Who's in charge here?!" the intense thirty-something officer asks with bluster.

"I'm Banks. I manage Cedar Island."

"Well, Mr. Banks, it sure doesn't seem like you manage it very well, does it now?" he hurls at the guide. "You lost the freakin' president!"

To his credit Banks doesn't tear the young prick's throat out. "My name's Banks, no mister in front, just Banks, and young fella I suggest you go sit somewhere comfortable and mind your manners because this is a lot bigger than your pay grade."

"That's right!" a commanding voice says, and we turn and see a three-star general emerge from one of the helicopters that just landed.

"I'm General Maxwell Swift, and we're taking command of the search-and-rescue operation. If you don't like it, son," he says to the lieutenant, "you can take it up with the Director of Homeland Security. Now who can tell me what happened?"

"Name's Banks, General Swift. If you come with Mr. Arnold and me, we'll fill you in. Your people can work with Cecil Johns inside the lodge to set up your base of operations."

The general radios his next in command, and we immediately see a cadre of men haul electronic communications equipment into the lodge.

Banks and I move down to the river's edge and give the three-star our account of what happened. Cecil Johns brings a large map of the Brule River Forest to us, and the general barks orders into his radio. Again we see men instantly leap into action. Two take our canoe and dump Bodie's and my gear on the river bank. They begin paddling downstream. Others follow with canoes they've commandeered from the estate. Then other men in uniform arrive, and an officer organizes the search. I know this is just the beginning. I look over at the general and Banks hopefully, and while they discuss the lay of the land, I step off to the side and call my commander-in-chief, Maggie.

Thankfully Maggie does not answer the phone because I dread telling her about Bodie being missing. I leave a vague message for her. "Hi honey, we've got a lot of action going on here. Just wanted to touch base with you. Give me a call when you get this message, okay?"

I look around the Cedar Island compound and can't believe the number of men scurrying around. So much for the pristine serenity of the Brule River Forest. Banks and I exchange glances, and I can tell from his expression that he's not a happy man.

"Well, I offered to help them conduct the search, but the general said he and his men would take care of things from now on. I tried to explain that I know every nook and cranny in this area, but my entreaty fell on deaf ears. His arrogance made me remember why Jake and I chose to muster out of the military a number of years ago. We saw far too many men die because of command's hubris. Sheriff Larabee tried to tell him he was making a mistake to dismiss my services, but I think the general just pictured another star on his uniform if he got the president back by himself."

An officer approaches the general to confirm that he has put roadblocks up at all major roads in the area. No traffic can get in, and none can get out, and check points have been established all along the Brule River from Cedar Island to the Winneboujou landing and the town of Brule.

Just then my phone rings, and I step a few feet away from Banks to answer what I expect will be the most difficult phone conversation I can remember. It's Maggie.

"Hey Maggie, we have a major problem here," I begin seriously.

"I'll say," she replies. "Tori and Mace and I were just watching the breaking news on television that the President of the United States is missing from a place called the Brule River Forest in Northern Wisconsin. Please tell me that you and Bodie aren't involved!"

"Well," I say somberly, "We are, honey," and then I just tell her everything about Bodie being with the president, and that we suspect they've been abducted by nefarious Russian agents. There is silence on the phone for a moment, and then I hear Maggie's voice transform into a baleful cry. "My baby! Clay Arnold, you said you'd keep him safe!" Then, more sobbing from the love of my life and the mother of our child.

"Maggie, Maggie, honey, I swear to you that we'll get him back safely."

"Oh Clay, how can this be happening? He's our little boy, Clay!"

My heart is breaking, and the only consolation I can offer my wife is that the military is on the scene, and that every boathouse, pump house, outhouse, and cabin will be searched. "We'll get him back, Maggie, I promise you."

"I'm coming up there, Clay," she says. "We need to find Bodie."

"I know, I know, honey, but this place is swarming with soldiers and cops, and I doubt that you could even fly into Duluth's airport with the security the authorities are putting in place. I'm heartsick about Bodie, but please let's let the police and the military do what they need to do."

The muted sobs I hear from her are devastating to me. "I promise to let you know the very minute we get any word."

Mace gets on the phone, and we talk seriously. "Oh Mace, this is another serious clusterfuck I need your assistance with. Seems like I'm always asking for you to help bail us out. Can you please try to look after things at home? I'm so sorry."

"Oh boy, what a mess!" Mace exhales. "I'll do my best, Clay. Tori too, but this is really scary."

"Tell me about it, Mace. I'm terrified for Bodie and the president. President Horvath is who the Russians are really interested in, and Bodie is pretty much expendable if push comes to shove."

Mace and I talk a little more, and I promise to keep everyone back home informed of developments. We disconnect, and I walk back over to join Banks. There must be a half-dozen helicopters swirling around the sky, and what was once a playground for presidents has become the site of a major military search operation. Banks and I each say a silent prayer that this search will bear fruit quickly, but neither of us is convinced that it will.

"C'mon, Clay!" Banks says. "There's not much else we can do right now. Let's head back up to the lodge and see what intel these guys come up with." I grab Bodie's and my gear from the river bank and follow the former marine inside the lodge. My hand grazes the inside of my jacket pocket, and I feel the reassuring shape of the Demon camera. I'm scared, and I'm pissed, and I can't wait to use it on someone deserving.

Chapter 21

RINA NEFSKY, a.k.a. Rini Neff, lounges in a deck chair by the boathouse with a book she pretends to be reading. The helicopters flying back and forth over the region have scattered the wildlife for ten miles in all directions. She does her very best to maintain her own composure knowing that the crushing weight of the American military is about to descend on her stretch of the Brule River.

Rini's encrypted phone chirps and damn near scares her out of her chair. "Yes?" she says evenly.

"I've been thinking," Mikhail Borodin says, and Rini exhales a breath of relief knowing that it's her handler and not anyone else.

"Yes?" she says again.

Mikhail continues, "Yes, I'm thinking that perhaps a little bit of misdirection might be useful to your extracting the big fish from under their noses, yes? Interesting to see which would prevail: Russian subterfuge or Yankee ingenuity."

"What do you have in mind?" she asks cautiously. "You know that these Americans will not rest until they get their president back."

"Of course you are right, Irina," he says using her Russian name. "That is why I think we need to make matters, uh, more challenging for the Americans, yes?"

Rini listens for several more minutes as Mikhail tells her his plan. He has her memorize a brief script of a conversation he wishes them to record together at the end of their phone call.

"After we record our little message, I will have it transmitted by our people so the Americans, who are surely utilizing every piece of technology to reveal any transmissions, will receive our ruse. We must keep it brief so it appears genuine. Say only what I have told you, nothing more. Is that understood, Irina?"

"Yes, I understand. And what of the boy?" she asks.

"Oh yes, the boy. Well, we both know that life can be cruel sometimes, yes? I will leave that to your discretion. Now then, let's record our message so we may test our subterfuge against their overrated ingenuity. Keep your phone nearby."

They record Mikhail's scripted message and disconnect. About five minutes pass.

Thump, thump, thump … a helicopter's rotors reverberate above. From her chair on the deck, Rini sees the gunship's armament trained on her location. She then sees two canoes carrying six men appear from a bend in the river. They're moving fast toward her dock, and Irina Nefsky practices every ounce of self-control that she can possibly muster.

"What's all of the commotion?!" she says with her practiced Midwestern accent. "Are you guys doing some sort of training maneuvers, or something?"

"Sorry to bother you, ma'am," a tough-looking young army ranger says. "We're helping the local authorities look for some fugitives," he fibs. "Have you seen anybody canoe by here in the past several minutes?"

"I've only just come out here," Rini says, "but I did see a canoe with two men canoeing very quickly as I was sitting down. They were moving so fast I thought maybe they were training for some kind of canoe race or something. They passed through here maybe five or ten minutes ago. Could they be the fugitives?" she asks with feigned fright.

The ranger instructs the men in the other canoe to continue downstream to try and overtake the Russian agents, and he radios the helicopter above them to continue scanning the river downstream.

"Sorry to bother you, ma'am, but we're checking every property in the area. We need you to cooperate with our search." The three rangers climb on to the deck, and Rini instantly feels very puny in comparison to the physical size of these guys. The one in command directs the other two to search the boathouse and surrounding forest and then meet him and the woman up at the cabin.

"My, my," Rini exclaims. "They must be dangerous criminals if you're going to all of this effort."

"Yes, ma'm," is the ranger's short reply. He brushes past her and heads up to the cabin. All the while he points his rifle from side to side, doing a serious search for any bad guys hiding near the path.

"Is this your place, ma'am?" he asks as they reach the cabin.

"I'm renting it for the summer," she replies. "Just moved in recently. I've been looking forward to having family join me, but with criminals on the loose I'm not so sure it's a good idea."

"Yes, ma'am," comes the ranger's standard reply.

They enter the cabin, and the other two rangers appear from the thick forest. The three of them do a thorough, coordinated search of the cabin's main and second floors. One floor below them the two Russian operatives listen intently in the dark to the heavy footfalls and muffled voices above. Viktor and Alexei know that if the American soldiers discover the trapdoor under the carpet that their asses are borscht. They quickly refill their syringes with more sedative in case the president or the boy begin to regain consciousness with the rangers above.

"Is there a basement?" he asks the woman as much to judge the timbre of her reply as the actual answer to his question.

"Yes, the door leading to the basement is in the kitchen."

The two other rangers receive a nod from their commander and go down the steps to search the basement. Less than a minute later they return shaking their heads no.

"Thank you, ma'am," the lead ranger says. "Here's a number for you to call if you see anything suspicious, anything at all." And just like that the three rangers exit the cabin, move down the path, and return to their canoe at river's edge.

"There's a lodge about six hundred feet downstream just above Wildcat Rapids," the commander states. "That's our next target to search, then we keep going, property by property, until we're ordered otherwise."

He radios to the control center at Cedar Island's lodge and reports that they've cleared the cabin and are moving down river.

Back in the cabin, Rini can barely maintain her stoic composure. The stress of the search finally gets to her. She watches the army rangers leave, then rushes to the bathroom, leans over the toilet, and retches.

Below the floor in the dark shelter, Jake Horvath regains semiconsciousness and tries to comprehend his predicament. His mind is still foggy from whatever sedative his assailants injected into him. He moves slightly and realizes that his wrists and ankles are bound. As his eyes adjust a little to the darkness, he senses he's not alone in the room. He wonders if it's the boy, Bodie. Then he hears Russian language being whispered, and he instantly recalls the struggle at the river. He chooses to remain still and bide his time.

Rini waits several minutes until she's confident that the soldiers are gone. Then she moves the table aside and slides the carpet away concealing the trapdoor. She speaks through the floor to Viktor and Alexei.

"I'm alone and opening the door. Do not shoot!"

She hears a muffled, "Dah," then opens the door and steps inside. She flips on the light switch, closes the trapdoor over her head, and climbs down the steps to the hidden room. It's dank with the smell of fear and sweat.

"They're still out, yes?" she asks about President Horvath and Bodie.

"Yes," Viktor replies, "but probably not for long. We have more sedative if we need it, or a couple of bullets if things get out of hand."

"You are not to shoot the president! Is that understood? If you do you sign your own death warrant because returning him alive to Moscow is the only thing the Kremlin will accept. Understand?!"

"Yes, Irina," Viktor responds. "What of the boy? I could kill him now, and no one would know until we are long gone."

"We keep him alive for now," she says. "The threat of harming him may be the only thing that keeps the president compliant, yes? We'll see how things go."

Jake Horvath listens to their plans with anger welling up inside him. His understanding of the Russian language isn't great, but he did study it for a semester many years ago. He understands enough though to realize their plan is not to assassinate him but to return him to Moscow for Badunov's thugs to debrief. He also knows that Bodie is very expendable to them. He fears for what they may do to the boy more than what they will likely do to him.

"There's something else, uh, Mr. Badunov has reportedly asked us to do," Rini begins quietly. "Apparently he has been very embarrassed for years at the breakup of the Soviet Union and the decline of Russia's influence worldwide. He wants to humiliate the West by stealing the president, but he also wants to humiliate Jake Horvath personally. For President Badunov, this is bloodsport. He wants us to take his finger and stick it in the face of the Americans."

"What means this?" Viktor asks naively for a murderous thug.

Just then Bodie begins to move. The sedative is wearing off. He stretches his hands and feet against his restraints, and his eyes flutter open. He is very confused by where he is and by the strangers around him. Then he sees the president, and he moans with fear as he remembers the attack on them at the river.

Alexei immediately slams his large hand over Bodie's mouth and smothers any further sound. He pulls his knife out and places it right in front of Bodie's eyes. "Now, Irina?" he asks.

"No, not yet," she directs, " but boy, you listen to me," she says menacingly. "One more sound out of you, and we will let you wander the woods without eyes, ears, or a tongue. Nod if you understand."

Bodie looks at the knife and at her with contempt and silently nods his head.

"Now then, Viktor, sever the president's finger before he wakes up and get something to control the blood. Take the pinky finger with the marine ring on it. The Americans will surely know we have their leader. Be quick. We have a ship to meet."

Bodie squirms against Alexei's meaty hands but remains quiet. Viktor takes his large ugly knife, kneels down in front of Jake Horvath, and grabs his left hand.

Before he can begin, Jake brutally brings his head forward and smashes his forehead into the bridge of Viktor's nose. It is a crushing blow that sends the Russian sprawling to the floor and momentarily disorients the president. With hands and feet bound, Jake springs toward Alexei and head butts his solar plexus. Alexei drops his knife. Viktor's eyes and face are awash with his own blood, but he manages to steady himself and leaps on top of the president's back. Bodie grabs Alexei's knife and swings awkwardly at the Russian and connects with his pant leg. He hears him scream, and it's the last sound that he hears as the Russian delivers a solid blow to his head rendering him unconscious.

Irina watches in fright as the violent ordeal unfolds and feels relief when she sees her two large Russian agents muscle Jake Horvath into submission.

"Hold his hand down, Alexei!" Viktor shouts, and the president makes one final attempt to free himself when he feels the agonizing sting of sharp steel against his flesh and bone and the wetness of his blood flowing from a bloody stump. "Aaarrraagghhh!"

The president's scream rouses Bodie into consciousness again, and he sees the President of the United States cradling his injured and bloody hand. He runs over to Jake and pulls out Weed's handkerchief that Tori gave him what seems like a lifetime ago now and firmly wraps it around Jake's stub to help staunch the flow.

"Give me the finger," Rini orders. "We have plans for it. You men can come upstairs now, but you must stay out of sight. No lights and no sounds, understood? Lock them down there and cover the trapdoor with the table and carpet. I have orders to leave now on a special assignment, but I should return in an hour or so."

The three Russians climb up the steps and lock the trapdoor. Bodie manages to find Alexei's knife which had been kicked away during the struggle. He cuts the thick duct tape that had bound his hands and feet and then does the same for the president.

"C'mon over to the sink, Jake, and lets get that wound cleaned up and put this towel around it."

Jake does as the boy suggests. He takes the Russian's knife from Bodie and hides it in his fishing vest.

"I'm really sorry they cut you, sir. Does it hurt much? It's all right if you want to cuss."

"Yeah, it hurts like a son of a bit ..." the President of the United States starts to say. Then he finishes his thought, "Thanks Bodie. You did really well, my friend. Now let's see if we can make life miserable for these jerks and find a way out of here."

Chapter 22

"GENERAL SWIFT, you're needed inside the lodge, sir," says an aide.

"What is it?" the general asks. "Anything from our search teams in the field?"

"Not yet, sir, but there appears to be some unusual chatter that the NSA picked up. They relayed it up to us, sir."

The general and his aide go inside the lodge, and Banks and I overhear their conversation and decide to follow them in.

"Trust me, Clay, they're not going to appreciate having civilians like us hanging around in here," Banks advises.

"Yeah, well, tell them to get my son back, and we can talk about it. Otherwise I'm staying."

Banks smiles wryly at my gumption, and we walk into the lodge's dining room which has been converted into a makeshift command center. We take up a position leaning against a rear wall.

"Let's hear what you've got, Lieutenant," the general says to his technology officer.

"It's relatively detailed and a little garbled. It's a conversation in Russian, presumably between a Russian agent operating in the states and her handler. The NSA places a high degree of certainty about that, sir."

They listen to the recording which has been translated into English, and then the general looks around the room at his men.

Banks and I stay silent and listen.

"Play it again, Jonesy," the general barks.

Jonesy plays the audio recording.

"So you have the big fish safely stashed away, yes?" the male Russian voice asks.

"Yes, he is safe and we have managed to avoid the, uh, other fishermen," the female Russian replies implying that the "other fishermen" are the American security forces. *"Is the ship ready, sir, to transport our catch?"*

"Yes, of course, just as we planned. I have chosen a secluded pier in Superior. All of the international sailing permits and documents have cleared customs."

"Which pier, sir?" the female operative asks.

"The trawler is named the Svetlana. She's moored at the end of Quebec Pier. Take U.S. highway 2 to U.S. route 53 and go over the Nemadji River and then drive past Hog Island. Turn right onto 21st Avenue and then left on Quebec Pier Road. Understand? You need to bring the big fish as soon as it is safe. Be very careful and hurry!"

"I understand fully," she says.

"That's it, General Swift. Nothing further, sir," the tech officer concludes.

General Swift paces the room contemplatively. "Any idea when that phone conversation occurred? How old is that message?"

The tech officer peers at his laptop looking at the report from the National Security Agency.

"It appears that conversation was made approximately ninety-five minutes ago. It took some time for the NSA to translate it and recognize that this was potentially a very critical message. Once they did, they contacted us immediately."

"Still they've got a good hour and a half lead on us. That boat could already be out of the harbor, and who says they even stay on that boat. They could be scheduling a rendezvous with a sea plane. We've got to move fast. Lieutenant, I need you to organize a full-scale effort to stop that ship from leaving Superior. Get the Wisconsin and Minnesota

National Guards to mobilize their forces, and I'll have more men sent in too if need be."

"Excuse me, General, I'm not so sure that's a very good idea," Banks offers evenly.

General Swift turns to face the fishing guide and says, "Who are you again, and why are you in here? I said get cracking, Lieutenant!"

"Belay that order, Lieutenant," Banks interjects insubordinately. "Who I am is a very close friend of Jake Horvath's and that boy is this man's son, and if you go in there like you're charging up San Juan Hill, they're both likely to die. Use a smaller force, General, no more than six men, preferably rangers or marines. But like you said, we've got to move fast."

General Swift looks directly into Banks's eyes. "You're army, aren't you?"

"No sir, a retired marine."

"Oh yeah, I think I know who you are now. Before he was elected president, Jake Horvath and a group of us used to meet for drinks periodically to tell war stories, and to try to forget them at the same time. The president used to tell us about this marine who served a couple of tours alongside him in Iraq and Afghanistan. Jake said he was like a brother and claimed this guy was the consummate warrior. He said this marine saved his ass on more than one occasion and saved a lot of brave boys' lives too. That's you, isn't it, Banks? I remember your face now from the photos President Horvath shared with us, and I recall him saying that you moved somewhere up in the North Woods."

"We did what we had to do, and I'm glad Jake and I survived it. Now we'd better get moving, sir."

General Swift takes Banks's counsel to heart, and he orders the lieutenant to select four men to join him.

"We're coming too!" Banks says pointing to himself and me.

"It's nonnegotiable, General," I add firmly. Banks gives a two-word reply, "Oorah that!"

"Get moving then dammit and bring 'em back!"

Two minutes later we're off the ground in a Lockheed AH 56 Cheyenne attack helicopter heading for Superior. The lieutenant offers Banks a handgun. He pats his hip and says, "Thanks, but I brought my own."

He offers me one as well and an extra clip which I gladly accept, and he asks if I need any instruction.

"No thanks, Lieutenant, I know how to handle one of these," I say. Instinctively my hand also goes to my pocket and feels the reassuring shape of my old friend, the Demon Camera.

Banks looks at me and asks, "I don't think I ever asked you if you were in the military, Clay."

"No, never was."

Banks continues, "Seems like you have some familiarity with weapons. I figured you were probably in the army or something. Maybe you're a collector."

"Oh, I'm a collector all right. Antique cameras, not firearms. Don't worry about me though, Banks, I've experienced my share of violence, and right now I'll do anything to get my son back safely."

"Yeah, and how do you feel about that?" Banks asks.

"I don't like it, and anymore I try to avoid violent conflict. Sometimes it's clearly justified though, and right about now I'm feeling mighty goddamn justified."

"Copy that! Let's go get them both!" Banks declares.

"We're fifteen minutes out," the pilot announces. "Everyone strap in. We're going in fast and low."

The *Svetlana* looms in front of us like an ominous gray iceberg as our helicopter approaches from the south. The pilot circles the dark-looking vessel to do a quick recon. Thankfully, no one shoots at us.

"Looks awfully quiet down there," the pilot reports. "Seems like the Russians picked a really secluded spot, and all they'd need to do is exit through the Superior Entry Channel and their ship would be in Lake Superior. A lot of water and a lot of ships to hide among between there and Canada."

"Put us down over there on the dock," the lieutenant orders. He eyes each of us. "Banks, you take Clay and two of my guys and approach the stern, and my men and I will go to the ship's bow. We'll meet midship if we don't encounter any resistance and go to the captain's quarters and then the wheelhouse."

We acknowledge his plan and slip out of the helicopter and run for the cover of large shipping containers on the dock.

"Awful darn quiet," Banks says to us. "I never like it when it's too quiet. C'mon let's try to keep to the containers' shadows and then get on board."

We only have about fifty feet to cover between us and the gangway, but it's an open dock between the shipping containers and the vessel. We could make easy targets. Banks leads the way by himself and runs the fifty feet crouched low with his gun pointing forward. He waves for us to follow one-by-one once he's by the stern. All I can think about is the safety of my son and hopefully getting the president back as well, but Bodie is the reason why I'm here. We all follow suit and join Banks.

He radios the lieutenant, "You see any movement? Any guards?"

"No, Banks, nothing. Makes me nervous."

"Yeah, me too. We're going up the gangway. Let's see if that draws some fire."

As we're about to move, we see a smaller vessel approach the *Svetlana* and two men begin hauling supplies and approaching our position by the stern.

"Whoa!" one of the guys blurts out when Banks quietly gets the drop on them and puts his pistol to one of the men's head.

"Down on the deck!" he tells them. "Down now!"

They don't need to be told twice. "Hey easy now," one of the sailors says. "We're just doing our job, and we don't have enough money on us to make it worth your while."

"What are you doing here?" Banks demands.

"Easy mister, we operate a ship chandlery business. Just bringing food and supplies, is all."

Banks frisks each of them and sees their work order.

"You're not delivering today," he says. "Now get out of here!"

The two men look up from their prone positions and see us standing over them with firearms trained at their heads. They don't need to be told twice this time either and cautiously get up and scamper back to their vessel. Banks radios the lieutenant and tells him about the ship suppliers. We watch for any other human movement on board the *Svetlana* and seeing none, we begin walking up the stern's gangway. Once on board, Banks directs the two soldiers to search the starboard side of the trawler while he and I take the port side. The lieutenant and his men clamber up the bow's gangway and split up to cover the ship's port and starboard sides as well.

"Nothing but seagulls and harbor mist," I say. "Maybe we got the wrong ship, Banks."

"Maybe," he acknowledges. "C'mon, let's try the captain's quarters. Someone's got to be home. Keep your head down and your eyes peeled."

The quiet is almost eerie, like it had been planned that way, but nothing else seems out of the ordinary. We meet the lieutenant and his men at midship.

The lieutenant says, "Let's try the captain's quarters, and if we don't find the president and the boy there, we'll split up with half of us going to the wheelhouse and the other half searching below deck."

We cautiously move forward as a unit with two men watching our backs at all times. We arrive at the captain's quarters, and Banks slowly pushes the door open. The lieutenant and his men enter first, and we follow. Nothing stands out at first, and then we see a small American flag on the captain's desk with a note: *"For our American friends."* Next to the note and flag is a clear plastic baggie. Banks picks it up and stares at its contents. I see his face flush red with anger as he seethes with rage. It's President Jacob Horvath's bloody pinky finger bearing his marine ring. The engraved gold words *Semper Fi* barely shine through a crimson stain.

Chapter 23

RINI NEFF'S EYES DART nervously from her SUV's rearview mirror to the road in front of her. She's just left the *Svetlana* docked at the Quebec Road pier after carrying out Mikhail Borodin's orders to the letter. All she wants to do now is return safely to the cabin and await further instructions from Mikhail about transporting the president to Russia. When her phone rings, she nearly runs her rented Highlander off the road as she fumbles to answer the call.

"So, how did your trip to Superior go, Rini?" Mikhail Borodin asks directly. "Did you deliver the, uh, package for the Americans?"

"Yes, I've done exactly as you instructed. I'm just now turning east on to U.S. Route 2 and heading back toward the town of Brule. I want to gas up my car there so we have plenty just in case."

"Very good, Rini. We sure don't want to risk running out of fuel if we need to change our plans. Now, listen closely …" and Mikhail takes the next couple of minutes explaining where she and her two operatives are to meet the ship that'll bring the president to Mother Russia.

"I understand," Rini says after Mikhail concludes his instructions. "And what of the boy?"

Mikhail thinks for a moment. "Keep him alive until we are safely out of American waters, then dispose of him." They disconnect their call.

Rini passes the exit for Amnicon Falls, and from out of nowhere she sees a military helicopter flying at her low and fast using the highway as its guide. She gasps as it approaches her position and only exhales as it soars past her presumably heading for the Quebec pier. She figures that she left the *Svetlana* with only a few minutes to spare. Too close for her comfort.

"I need to find a new line of work," she mumbles to herself.

At this point it's been impossible to keep word of the president and Bodie's abductions in Northern

Wisconsin a secret. Leaks naturally occur when so many people are involved. News of the presidential abduction goes viral, and within an hour virtually the entire world is aware of Russia's brazen assault on America.

From Washington to Moscow and Beijing to London, the phone lines are on fire with questions, threats, and denials. When Vice President Trevor Wentworth calls Moscow demanding to speak with Vladimir Badunov directly, he is told that their fearless leader is busy watching the news on television and can't come to the phone. Mr. Badunov is literally and figuratively giving the finger to America!

Back home in Indiana Maggie, Mace, and Tori are terrified by the sketchy reports that news crews are delivering. News anchors pose many questions, but chief among them are: *Is the president alive? Who is this boy with him? Where is the Brule River, and why is the president there? Did the Russians really assault the president or was it some rogue fringe group? And most of all, who's in charge in Washington?*

Maggie is beside herself with fear, and she attempts to call me. Unfortunately her call vibrates on my phone as Banks and the two rangers and I are searching the trawler. Not a good time to answer the phone, even for Maggie. I'll call her back later.

The heartache that I feel after we search the *Svetlana* and come up with only a bloody stub of a finger is demoralizing. I am so worried about Bodie and beyond frustrated that I'm powerless to help my son. Banks hangs his head low thinking about his close friend, Jake, being tortured by thugs and still being held in their clutches.

"Hang in there, buddy," Banks says to himself. "No man left behind."

After we search every inch of the trawler, the lieutenant radios General Swift to tell him what we found. The general explodes with creative curses and contacts the White House and the Joint Chiefs of Staff. Within minutes America is on high alert and armed warheads are brought into full readiness in Europe, Japan, South Korea, and both coasts of the United States.

"There's not much else we can do here in Superior," the lieutenant informs the general. "Seems to me that this rush to the *Svetlana* was meant as a diversion and as a brazen insult. Any more intel from our search teams?"

"We're turning over every rock in that damn stream from Cedar Island to the town of Brule with nothing to show for it yet. I want you men to get back here ASAP, especially Banks. I still have a feeling the Russians are holding the president in the Brule River Forest, and no one knows that area better than Banks."

"Roger that," the lieutenant says. "We'll be back in twenty minutes, sir."

———

Rini Neff begins to relax a little with each mile that she drives away from the *Svetlana* and the town of Superior. She knows they have stirred up the hornet's nest, but the American hornets haven't managed to sting her team yet. She maintains a speed just under the posted limit and cruises through small towns along U.S. Route 2 with the colorful names of Poplar, Maple, and Blueberry. Several minutes later she arrives at the bustling metropolis of Brule, population 663 people, and pulls into the parking lot for the gas station and grocery store across the road from Marna's Place. Everywhere she looks she sees men and women in uniform and members of news crews.

"Please do not fail us, Mikhail!" she mumbles to herself, but she is well aware that in their world of espionage all souls are expendable.

Rini exits her Highlander by a gas pump and notices a slight tremor in her hands as she anxiously begins filling her tank. Even though she's a seasoned veteran at spy-craft, all Rini has to do is look around at the staggering number of people in the small town of Brule to know her life is very tenuous now. Military personnel, law enforcement officers, news staffs, and, of course, curiosity seekers are everywhere.

As Rini finishes filling her gas tank, she's visibly startled when she hears a familiar voice call her name. She turns in the direction of the voice and sees Marna and her daughter, Perrin, exit the grocery store with sacks of food and provisions for the diner.

"Hi there, Rini," Marna says, "I thought that was you. Sorry if I surprised you."

"Oh hello, Marna," Rini replies trying to recapture her emotional equilibrium. "And Perrin, too. How nice to see you both. Perrin, are you helping out your mother and sister at the diner with all of these people around here?"

"Hi Rini. Yes, I am," Perrin says. "Mom and Sarah asked if I could help out a little in the kitchen with all of the turmoil going on with the president's abduction. So, we closed the real estate office down for a couple of days. It's not likely anyone will be interested in real estate while we have all of this commotion going on anyway."

"Dah," Rini responds, "Awful thing the president and that poor little boy getting taken. Alas, these things happen."

Both Marna and Perrin are a little surprised by Rini's off-handed attitude about the President of the United States being abducted.

"Yeah well, things like this don't happen around here, Rini," Marna returns. "And he is the president after all."

"Dah," Rini replies again without any attempt to hide her accent.

"So, how're things working out for you at the cabin so far?" Perrin asks. "Are you feeling settled in?"

"Yes, it's a lovely place although with all of the soldiers running around, it isn't as peaceful as I was hoping for."

"Did your brothers show up for a visit like you were expecting?" Perrin asks.

"Yes, they have. I'm going to meet them now, and we are thinking about taking a drive toward the Apostle Islands just to get away from all of this hullabaloo. Do I just drive on Route 2 to get there?"

"You can do that," Marna replies, "and that'll take you to Ashland, but you can take Route 13 instead and drive along the coast through Cornucopia, and you'll end up in Bayfield which is lovely this time of year. The Apostle Islands are right there."

"Dah? What is a cornucopia? Is that someone's name?"

Both Marna and Perrin laugh. "No, it's a thing, not someone's name. It means 'horn of plenty'. It's more symbolic than real though."

"Actually, we're supposed to meet some friends around there, and I remember they mentioned a little town named Cornucopia," Rini offers.

"Really?!" Perrin says quizzically. "It's a tidy little community, but there's not much there. A few stores and restaurants, Fullerton's Fisheries, and a print shop that our friend Joel Cooperman owns. Heck, only about a hundred people live in Cornucopia. I'm surprised you're meeting anyone around there."

"Me too," Rini replies, "but that was our friends' suggestion. Sorry, but I must run now. It was good seeing you both." She abruptly climbs back in her Highlander, closes the car door, and starts the engine.

"Did that conversation with Rini strike you as a little odd?" Marna asks Perrin as they watch her drive away.

"Yeah, Mom, it struck me as a little unusual too, but we probably shouldn't be too surprised considering she came here for a peaceful vacation along the Brule River, and we end up with a major crush of humanity descending on us."

"I guess you're correct, Perrin, but still, something doesn't seem quite right. Maybe it's her hard-to-place hint of an accent too. It's not like the

Scandinavian accents we're accustomed to. My sense is that she also seems more guarded rather than just annoyed with the increase in people. Did she strike you as being unusual in any way when you showed her the Stine cabin?"

"No, not really, Mom, but I was pretty eager to finally have that property produce some income rather than just sitting empty. She seemed fine, but a little different. But heck, you live up here in Douglas County virtually your whole life, and any outsider is going to seem different."

"I suppose you're right," Marna says thoughtfully. "Anyway, let's get these supplies to Sarah before she runs out of food for everyone. I hope you can stay and help your sister and me."

"Of course, Mom. We stick together!"

Chapter 24

JAKE AND BODIE EACH examine their predicament locked as they are in a windowless subterranean room in an older building that they have no recollection of being brought to.

"Where are we, sir?" Bodie asks Jake, "and who are these people, and how do we get out of here?"

"As to where we are, Bodie, I'm really not sure. It's hard to say how long we were unconscious after they drugged us. We could be anywhere. I'm fairly certain that they're people working with the Russian government. As to how we get out of here, we can only bide our time and wait for an opportunity to fight back and run."

"Gee, swell, Mr. President!" Bodie replies sarcastically. "Let's take another look at your hand, sir. We need to keep that wound clean."

Jake marvels at the maturity that his young friend is showing given his age and the frightful situation they're in. Jake and Bodie stand over the sink as Bodie unwraps the towel from Jake's hand. Due to the direct pressure the president applied, the wound has stopped flowing as freely but still oozes some blood. Together they wash the president's injured hand and find other clean towels in the cabinet below the sink. They also find an ancient-looking first aid kit and check the expiration date on the tube of topical antibiotic contained inside: February, 1999. The ointment is woefully out of date, but thankfully it was never opened. Bodie gently applies some to the president's finger, and they re-wrap it in a visually clean washcloth.

"Hold still, sir, while I tie this piece of cord around the cloth to hold it in place.

"That's much better, Bodie, thanks! You'd make a great medic."

Jake examines every inch of the room that holds them. No windows, only the trapdoor over their heads as an exit, a sink and a toilet, and a couple of chairs. Jake falls back on his marine training and assesses what he and Bodie can use as weapons. Not much. The president lifts the ceramic lid off of the toilet tank and sets it by the foot of the steps leading up. He wrenches the ballcock loose and figures he can use its metal rod as a gouging weapon, plus they have the knife hidden in Jake's fishing vest that the Russian lost in their fight.

"Let's take inventory of what else we can also use as weapons in our vests, Bodie. We won't have anything that compares with their guns, but maybe we can surprise them with something."

They begin emptying their vest pockets, and aside from several flies, their forceps, and landing nets, they find precious little else. Bodie stares at their collection of stuff and takes one of their fishing nets and begins attaching the hooks of individual flies into the strings of the net. When he's done he has about twelve hooks attached to the landing net. Jake hides the snapped-off ballcock from the toilet and manages to partially conceal it up his right shirt sleeve.

"Let's see if we can get these guys to make some mistakes," Jake says to Bodie. "You stand behind the stairs with the lid to the toilet tank, and if we can get them to come down here, see what damage you can do to him, and I'll take it from there, okay?"

"Ummm …" Bodie stammers. "I'll do my best, sir, but I'm really scared."

"Yeah, me too," President Horvath admits honestly, "but we've got each other. Let's mess with their heads and see if we can catch them off guard. Make a lot of racket, Bodie, okay?!"

In unison Bodie and Jake begin howling at the top of their lungs: "Let us out of here! We're being held prisoner. Help, anyone! Help! Oooorrrrraaaahhhhh!"

Jake silently climbs the steps until he crouches at the very top.

Viktor and Alexei nearly fall out of their chairs from the loud tumult coming from under the floor. Alexei goes over to the rug concealing the trapdoor and begins stomping his foot.

"Shut up down there!" he booms. "Quiet!"

Jake and Bodie continue their hollering, and Viktor joins Alexei by the trapdoor.

"Go down there and shut them up, Alexei. If the Americans hear them, we're finished!"

Alexei pulls the table and rug away and shouts through the floor. "Shut up and move away from the stairs. I'm coming down there!" He kneels down and lifts the handle and pulls the door open a crack so he can peer down and see where their captives are. Immediately he receives a vicious stab to his forehead from the metal rod of the ballcock. The Russian recoils in pain and feels a trickle of blood fall onto his eyebrow. He explodes with a string of Russian curses and slams the trapdoor shut.

Viktor looks at the blood on his comrade's face and shakes his head mockingly.

"So, you can't even make it down the steps, Alexei? That American president is too much for a strong man like you, eh? Here, let me show you how to do this simple thing," he laughs derisively.

Viktor bends down and opens the trapdoor with his 9mm Makarov pointed in front of him. He steps inside and immediately sees the president standing against the wall about eight feet in front of him. Jake has a slight smile on his face and extends his injured hand and motions for Viktor to come forward. Being armed with a pistol Viktor is more than willing to teach this American dog a few lessons. He takes two steps down the stairs, and Bodie leaps from behind the steps and slams the porcelain toilet tank lid against Viktor's unprotected knees.

Viktor explodes with a shriek as he falls forward from the steps and crashes to the floor in front of Jake. Somehow he manages to hang on to his pistol. Jake leaps on Viktor and attempts to wrestle the gun away, but the Russian grabs his injured hand and wrenches the finger stub painfully. Viktor rolls on top of Jake and is about to pistol-whip his face when Bodie charges up from behind with his landing net and crams it over Viktor's head and face and yanks on it savagely. The hooks from the dozen or so dry flies Bodie had attached to the net dig into the Russian's face and head like a swarm of killer bees. Viktor howls in pain and kicks Bodie away. Alexei comes charging down the steps. He looks at his comrade's bloody face as Viktor lets go of the president and tries to pluck the excruciating hooks from his face.

Jake is immediately on his feet, but he stops dead in his tracks when he hears a gunshot ricocheting off the room's stone floor and walls. Alexei points his gun directly at Bodie's head and screams, "Cease or the boy dies!" Jake winces and backs off.

Rini turns off of State Route 27 onto the gravel lane leading to her cabin. She's just returning from gassing up her car in Brule when she pulls up to the cabin and hears the gunshot. She scrambles out of her car and runs for the cabin. When she gets inside she sees the table and carpet pulled away from the trapdoor with the odor and bluish haze of gun smoke coming from the room below. She cautiously approaches the steps leading down and sees Alexei holding a gun on the president and the boy. Blood is dripping from his forehead.

"What is this?!" Rini bellows at the two Russian men. "I leave you for a couple of hours, and you get into a brawl with a wounded man twenty years older than you and shoot off a gun. What did I tell you about remaining quiet? Surely someone may have heard that sound, and if so, I will be very pleased to tell the Kremlin it was you two idiots."

Rini now has her gun drawn too, and she looks more closely at Viktor.

"What are those? Fish hooks in a net? You look like a dumb bull that got tangled in barbed wire! You two get upstairs and get those damn things out of your face. And you, Mr. President, make sure that you mind your manners. Your journey is far from over, and I plan to get you to our destination in one piece. Whether the boy makes it or not is up to you." She turns and climbs up the steps, locks the trapdoor, and replaces the rug and table.

After Rini leaves, Bodie runs to the president's side, and Jake slumps against the boy. Bodie notices blood seeping from the president's side.

"I don't think it's serious, Bodie, but that ricochet took a little hide out of my side."

"Here, sir, let me take a look." Sure enough, it was just a flesh wound, but Bodie knew he had to get it cleaned and then apply some of that antiseptic and a dressing on it of some sort. Thankfully, old man Stine had left a first aid kit in his bomb shelter albeit some twenty-odd years ago.

"We need to use what we've got," Bodie says evenly.

"Copy that, my friend. Oh, and by the way, Bodie, good going with that toilet tank lid and the fish net. I wouldn't want to go into battle against you."

Bodie beams with pride, and the two warriors huddle together discussing strategy.

Chapter 25

WHEN OUR HELICOPTER lands back at Cedar Island, the lieutenant goes inside the lodge to debrief the general about our disheartening search of the *Svetlana*. Banks and I walk down to the Brule River trying to figure out next steps.

Banks calls his long-time friend Sheriff Muggs Larabee to give him an update. Once the military and other officials arrived at Cedar Island, the local county sheriff was pretty much cut out of the flow of information.

"Are you picking up any scuttlebutt from the locals, Muggs?" Banks inquires.

"No, not really, Banks, but we're keeping our eyes and ears open, and I have a few of my officers stationed at various checkpoints in the county."

With Banks on the phone, I take the opportunity to call Maggie back. It's not a conversation I'm looking forward to.

Maggie answers the phone immediately. "Clay! Please tell me you have good news about Bodie!"

"Nothing yet, honey, everyone is searching high and low."

I debate to tell her about our search of the *Svetlana* but see no point in sharing the gruesome news about the president's finger, so I opt not to broach the subject. I try to be as reassuring to Maggie as possible, but it's hard to do when I'm not feeling the least bit reassured myself.

"Honey, I need to go now. We're going to keep searching until we bring Bodie and the president back safely. I know this is awful, but I promise you we'll do everything humanly possible to get them back. I'll let you know as soon as I have something to report."

Both Banks and I end our phone calls around the same time. We stand at the river's edge and stare vacantly at the water as it drifts by. Banks is about to speak when he hears a familiar, foreboding sound and looks to the north in the river's direction. It's a solitary gunshot, and from its sound he recognizes it as coming from a pistol rather than a rifle or shotgun. A few moments later he witnesses a flock of crows and other birds streaming over our heads from that direction. Banks calls Agent Blackburn, the new leader of the president's disgraced security detail, to see if he heard the shot and knows anything about it.

"Yeah, I heard it too," Agent Blackburn confirms. "We've got two teams canoeing and searching in that area, but they haven't come up with anything yet. We're not sure who fired that round, sir."

"Keep looking, Blackburn. The boy's father and I are going to head downstream and do more of our own searching. Tell your trigger-happy guys not to shoot our asses."

"Copy that, Banks. Keep us in the loop."

As soon as they disconnect Banks's phone rings again, and he sees that it's a call from his good friend, Marna Philips.

"Hmm, wonder what she wants," he muses out loud to himself. "Hey there, Marna, what's going on? We're pretty busy right now."

"No doubt!" she says emphatically. "Where are you, Banks? Are you at Cedar Island now?"

"Yeah, me and the boy's father. The military and security people have taken over the lodge, and Clay and I are looking for any clues we can find. You got something for us?"

"Don't know," she replies honestly. "Just a weird gut feeling I have that I wanted to get your reaction to."

"Tell me, Marna."

Over the next minute Banks listens intently as Marna describes a niggling feeling she has about this woman with a funny accent that she served at her diner. She tells him about Perrin and her running into this woman named Rini at the gas pump and about her unusual demeanor. Marna explains that Perrin rented the old Stine place to her just above Wildcat Rapids.

"And what does Perrin think?" Banks asks.

"Well, neither of us is exactly sure what to think. We could be dead wrong, but we both agree that this woman's behavior strikes us as a little unusual. I tried to reach Sheriff Larabee but had to leave a message for him. You're the only other person I thought to call, Banks."

"I really appreciate the heads-up, Marna. We're racing against the clock here, and honestly while they could be anywhere by now, I still think they're holed up somewhere along the Brule. Clay and I are going to canoe downstream and see what we can find. I really appreciate the call, Marna."

"You bet, Banks, and quit being such a stranger at my place. I've missed seeing your handsome face and hearing your snarky-ass witticisms."

"Yeah, yeah," Banks replies, and they hang up.

"What did she say, Banks?" I ask. "I only heard bits and pieces of your conversation. Do we have a lead?!"

"Maybe," he says. "C'mon let's get in my canoe and paddle downstream. There's a place I want us to check out."

Banks and I climb into the canoe, with me in the bow and Banks in the stern. As Banks pushes off from the landing, he thinks back on the single gunshot he heard a little earlier and the flight of birds he saw coming from downstream.

"Stay sharp," he says aloud. He guides their canoe into the Brule's swift current and enters the Falls Rapids just below Cedar Island.

Mikhail calls Rini on their secure phones. No intentionally fake telephone transmissions this time for the ever-listening Americans.

"So Irina? How are things going with our, uh, guests? Are you ready to test our Russian subterfuge against their overrated Yankee ingenuity again?"

"Of course, Mikhail. You should know though that while I was traveling to the *Svetlana* and back, Alexei and Viktor got into an altercation with the president and the boy. Both of my men were injured, and the idiots shot a gun off, but I arrived just in time and got things back under control. We're ready to move when you give the word."

Mikhail's jocular demeanor hardens, and he seethes thinking that Rini's undisciplined men could jeopardize the operation.

"I thought you said these men are pros, Irina," Mikhail says icily. "You tell them from me, 'no more mistakes, none!' Was the president hurt?"

"I've already told them in no uncertain terms, Mikhail, but I will be more than happy to share your admonition as well, sir. The president appears to be okay, with the exception of getting a bit roughed up and missing his little finger of course."

"You would do well to keep him in decent shape, Irina, in case the Kremlin wishes to parade our catch in front of the world. Heaven forbid we would look uncivilized if the president appears before the news cameras looking all maimed and disfigured. And, the boy? What of him? Is he still alive?" Mikhail asks.

"Yes, for now. Threatening the boy's life is about the only thing that gives us control over the president. We can always dispose of him once we're on board the ship, or we can just kill him and hide his body in the bomb shelter below the floor."

"You're a clever woman, Rini. I'll leave that decision up to your discretion. Now then, let's discuss specifically where I want you to meet our real transport ship. It will be dark soon, and any cover we can get will be helpful."

The two veteran Russian agents take the next few minutes discussing the location of their rendezvous point in Siskiwit Bay.

"From your location I figure you're about thirty or forty minutes away, Irina. The ship will be dark. Just approach the stern end, and you will be met. Safe travels, old friend. I look forward to drinking a toast to your success in Cornucopia."

Rini and Mikhail disconnect their call, and she approaches Alexei and Viktor. The latter's face is puffy and red with spots of drying blood from where Alexei yanked Bodie's hooks out of Viktor's face and head.

"Lovely!" she says sarcastically. "Just so you know, I told Mikhail about your brawl with the president and the boy. As you might imagine, he was not pleased."

The two Russian toughs look sheepishly at the floor.

"Now then," she says. "We will wait just a little bit longer until it's dark, and then we leave. Alexi, prepare the sedatives for the dart gun. No sense getting into another brawl with the president and a little boy. After the sedatives take effect, you'll carry the president and boy upstairs and load them in my SUV. Then, conceal them both under blankets."

"Are you sure you want to take the boy too, Rini?" Viktor asks. "I could kill him now, and we could just leave him here."

Rini ponders for a moment. "Yes, we could do that, Viktor, but I think we should keep him alive for now, at least until we arrive at the ship. Then, you may dispose of him, but not until then, understand?"

"Dah," he replies. "Yes, I understand."

The sun is getting lower in the western sky as Banks navigates our canoe through the Falls Rapids. If it weren't for the terrifying reality of the situation, I would enjoy the river's scenery as the light reflects off the water and tree shadows grow longer in the ebbing daylight. I'd give anything to have Bodie with me plying these waters on a warm summer evening, anything, but now a retired marine who I barely know and I are engaged in a frantic search to save loved ones. Necessity does indeed breed strange bedfellows.

Banks guides us out of the Falls Rapids, and as darkness descends on the Brule, he expertly takes us through Little Twin Rapids, Big Twin Rapids, and Sucker Lake. Now the broad, dark expanse of Big Lake looms in front of us. Banks paddles us over to the shoreline under the protective branches of an overhanging cedar tree. We both sit still and look for any motion or any sound that doesn't seem natural.

"There are only a couple of lodges along Big Lake," Banks whispers to me. "I know the owners well enough, and Sheriff Larabee told me that between his deputies and the army's men, they've pretty much dismissed them as potential hiding places."

"So, what are we doing out here, Banks, if they've already been ruled out?" I say with frustration.

"My conversation with Marna leads me to believe otherwise, at least about one property in particular. It's at the north end of Big Lake a couple of hundred yards above Wildcat Rapids. I'm going to keep us close to the shoreline for protective cover, especially with the moon starting to rise. Let me do the canoeing now, Clay. Less chance of noise from our paddles."

Banks pushes our canoe away from the river bank, and we begin to drift into Big Lake. No one else is on the water at this time, and I scan the deepening shadows for any signs of life. Banks paddles us cautiously from one protective spot to another, and before long he guides us over to the shoreline again and holds our canoe still as we listen in the darkness to the Brule River's steady rhythm.

"The old Stine lodge is just up ahead about fifty yards," he states. "Marna told me that she and her daughter, Perrin, have an uneasy feeling about the woman renting the place for the summer. It's been abandoned for a while until Perrin rented it to her recently. I learned a long time ago to trust Marna's instincts. Perrin's too. I suggest we get out here and go the rest of the way on foot, Clay. Let's keep to the shadows and stay very quiet."

I nod my head in acknowledgement. I have no idea what we'll find at this lodge, but I have no other practical option than to trust this river guide's instincts as well. I have my handgun drawn and feel the reassuring presence of the Demon camera in my vest pocket.

Chapter 26

RINI NODS HER HEAD to Alexei and Viktor. "It's time. The two of you go down there and sedate the president and the boy. I'll bring the SUV around so it's closer to the porch, and I'll get the blankets ready. Understand?"

"Dah," they say in unison. Rini leaves, and Alexei inserts a cartridge of sedative into the dart gun. He places a second one in his pocket and nods that he's ready to Viktor. They remove the table and carpet concealing the trapdoor, and Alexei kneels down and throws open the door while Viktor keeps his pistol trained on the opening. Alexei places his feet on the top step, and he bends down to see

his targets. He sees the president and the boy calmly sitting next to each other against the far wall.

"Ah, such a touching sight," he says sarcastically. "The great American president needs a boy to protect him," he taunts.

The president chooses not to dignify the ignorant comment coming from a man that he knows the American government will hunt for as long as it takes and finally assassinate regardless of whether the president lives or dies.

"Get on with it, Alexei!" Viktor exhorts. "Do your job before Rini returns."

Jake stands and plants his feet firmly on the ground. Alexei moves quickly down the steps holding the dart gun, and Viktor follows him immediately with his pistol aimed forward. They both notice blood seeping from the president's side where he'd caught the bullet's ricochet.

"Do it now, Alexei!" Viktor urges.

Alexei aims the dart gun at the president's torso, and just as he pulls the trigger, Bodie leaps in front of Jake and feels the stab of the dart in his chest. The president screams, "Noooo!!!" as Bodie staggers a couple of feet, tries to pull the dart out of his chest, and falls in a heap. Out cold.

"You, bastards!" Jake hurls at the Russians, and he kneels down to check on his young friend laying at his feet.

"Oh, you would prefer we use a real bullet, eh Mr. President?!" Viktor taunts Jake.

Alexei quickly inserts the second sedative cartridge into the dart gun and pulls the trigger just as Rini appears at the trapdoor's opening.

The dart bites into Jake's neck, and he tries one final noble leap at his assailant as the drug courses through his veins and renders him unconscious.

"Quickly now!" Rini says to the men. "Bring the president first, and then Viktor you guard him while Alexei comes back for the boy. We must hurry. The ship is waiting!"

Viktor and Alexei manhandle the president up the steps to the main level. They catch their breath for a moment and then grabbing Jake Horvath's ankles and wrists, they unceremoniously haul his limp frame out to the SUV and shove him inside.

"Get the boy, Alexei, quickly now," Rini exhorts. "And you, Viktor, don't you dare take your eyes off of the president for even one second, understand?!"

"Dah," Viktor mumbles through lips made swollen from ripping Bodie's dry flies out of his face. Alexei returns a minute later carrying the unconscious boy over his shoulder. He dumps Bodie inside the rear of the SUV with the president. Rini carefully conceals their motionless bodies beneath a heavy blanket and tarpaulin.

"Quickly now!" she directs. "I'll drive. Alexei, you ride up front with me. Viktor you stay in back and keep an eye on our passengers."

As they pull away from the cabin, Irina Nefsky gives it a final glance. "How nice it would be to live in such a place someday," she thinks wistfully. Then she thinks of Mikhail Borodin and the ship waiting for them at a dock in Cornucopia. Rini's professional instincts gleaned from years of Russian spy-craft kick in, and she accelerates out of the cabin's lane onto State Route 27 north.

"How are they, Viktor?" Rini asks.

"Sleeping like babies," he replies.

"Good, keep them well hidden, and make sure you have more sedative ready, yes?!"

"Dah, Irina."

The traffic on State Route 27 is virtually nil. They see more deer than they do cars. Rini looks at her watch and sees that it's nearly 11:00 PM, and she's starting to breathe a little easier until she looks ahead at the junction of County Road B and State Route 27. Lights are flashing from a patrol car that is turned sideways blocking the road a hundred yards in front of her.

Rini instantly slows the SUV and barks, "We have company. It looks like two policemen. I'll have to stop for them. Act naturally but have your silenced weapons ready."

She approaches the roadblock at a respectful speed. A uniformed county deputy holds his hand up indicating for them to stop. Rini complies. She rolls down her window and smiles at the officer.

"Evening, ma'am, can I see your driver's license and registration?"

As Rini fumbles through her purse looking for her wallet, the other officer flashes his light inside the car and sees Viktor and Alexei sitting calmly. He spies stuff covered by a tarpaulin in the space behind Viktor. The officer walks around to the rear of the car to get a better look at its concealed contents. As Rini hands the SUV's rental papers to the officer, Alexei and Viktor nod at each other.

The officer at the rear of the vehicle lifts up the handle on the Highlander's tailgate and peers inside at the large covered bundle. Viktor turns in his rear seat to face the officer and casually shakes his head "No."

The officer begins to call out to his partner to join him when Viktor points and pulls the trigger of his silenced Markarov. The bullet tears into the hapless officer's forehead stealing the light of life from his eyes. The officer taking Rini's papers hears the distinctive sound of the silencer and turns in that direction when Alexei reaches his arm in front of Rini and pulls his trigger through her open window. Both officers are mortally wounded.

"Quickly you two! Get their bodies off the road and move their car to the side," Rini shouts.

They leap into action immediately, and a minute later they're back in their car driving north on Route 27 four miles south of the town of Brule. The strobing lights of the officers' squad car flash brightly in the silent night for an audience of none.

"That was close," she said. "You men performed very well. How are the passengers doing? Still sleeping?"

"Yes, still asleep. How much longer until we reach the ship?" Viktor asks.

"Not far. Perhaps thirty minutes. I need to observe the speed limits though. We don't want to get stopped again. We should arrive around midnight."

Chapter 27

BANKS STEADIES THE canoe as I step out on to the river bank. He waits a moment to listen to the forest sounds as the sun goes down, and then he joins me.

"This way," he says as he finds a deer path leading through the woods toward the cabin. From this distance we can see no lights on at the cabin, and the only sound we hear is the quickening flow of the Brule as it approaches Wildcat Rapids. Through the trees I can faintly see the spectral shape of a large wooden structure looming in the near distance. I say a silent prayer that Bodie is here and safe.

Fortunately for us the forest surrounds the cabin, and we are able to come within fifteen yards of it well hidden.

"You stay here," Banks directs. "I want to scout around the perimeter to see what I can find before we try entering the cabin."

I nod my compliance, but I don't like being left behind despite my knowing that Banks is a seasoned marine.

Banks notices my reticence to stay behind and says, "Clay, I mean it. Stay here. There's too much at stake. I'll return in a minute."

Again, I nod my compliance and reluctantly kneel down behind some bushes to wait for him to complete his surveillance.

A moment later Banks disappears in the dark forest like a wraith. He walks quietly on the sandy earthen soil stopping every ten feet or so to look and listen. Nothing. He comes to the parking area next to the cabin and sees tire tracks and a pickup truck. The tracks look fresh and the truck's hood is cool to the touch. He looks inside the truck and is surprised to see the electrical wiring ripped loose from the steering column. Clearly, someone didn't want this truck being used.

Banks moves away from the truck to a place in the trees with a good view of the porch entrance. Again, he looks and listens for any activity from within the cabin. Nothing. He stays within the protective cover of the trees as he returns to my position. One second I'm alone, and the next he's kneeling next to me in the loamy soil.

"It's very quiet," he says. "There's a pickup parked on the other side, but someone sabotaged the wiring. The tire tracks indicate there was another vehicle too, but it's gone. Let's go inside. Stay behind me and do exactly as I say." He leads the way.

I can't help but think of the many clandestine operations I conducted as an avenging vigilante over the years. Stealth was always my modus operandi, but given how terrified I am that Bodie is in the hands of very desperate people makes me feel somewhat relieved that I'm with an experienced warrior like Banks.

He and I cautiously approach the steps leading to the cabin's porch. Banks holds his hand up for me to wait as he examines the soil around the steps looking for wires or any other telltale signs of a booby trap or silent alarm. A few moments later he motions for me to follow as we walk up the steps and enter the porch. The rusty hinges and spring on the screen door screech their resistance, and I cringe hoping that our position hasn't been compromised. Banks moves quickly now, and we stand in the cabin's living room with nothing to be heard except our breathing and the beating of our hearts.

"Stay here," he says to me again, and again he swiftly disappears to surveil the rest of the cabin. I crouch behind a large arm chair and listen in the dark. A couple of very long minutes pass, and Banks suddenly reappears at my side as silently as he'd left.

"I think we're alone," he says, and he reaches over to a table and turns on a lamp. I'm immediately disoriented by the light.

"What do you think?" I ask hopefully. "Do we even know that they were here?"

"No," he replies honestly, "but I can't imagine why anyone would rip the wiring out of the truck unless they were up to something nefarious."

"Shit!" I mutter growing even more agitated about my son's fate. "They could be anywhere, Banks. Even if they were here, we don't have a clue where they are now."

I stare down at my feet dejectedly and glance around the room absently. I picture Maggie's face and can't even begin to think what our life would be like without Bodie. Tears of anguish and fear and anger come to my eyes. I stare at the floor some more and notice something that seems oddly out of position. The area carpet and a small table are haphazardly out of place, and the lamp on the table is sitting askew. I walk over to straighten them when I notice a handle set into the floor.

"Hey Banks, take a look at this," I say. He strides over and bends down for a closer look. He moves the table off of the carpet and folds the area rug back. "It's a trapdoor," I announce stating the obvious.

A new wave of anxiety hits me as I ponder what or who could be below the floor.

Banks pulls the handle and opens the door in the floor. He sees a light switch and flips it on revealing a hidden room. We both descend down the wooden steps and see an empty room with a couple of chairs, a sink, and a toilet with a part of its plumbing ripped loose. A broken tank lid and paper wrappers from gauze and bandages lie scattered on the floor.

"What the …?!" I begin. "What is this place?" I ask.

Banks looks as surprised as I feel trying to comprehend who had occupied this room. "Were Jake and Bodie even here?" he wonders aloud. We look at each other forlornly.

We're about to head back up the steps when I notice a blue rag lying on the floor near the sink. I walk over to throw it in the trash when a pang of recognition hits me.

"Banks!" I say. "This is Bodie's handkerchief. Our friend, Tori, gave it to him for our trip. It belonged to her brother, Weed, who was like a brother to me."

We both examine the handkerchief closely and see that it's caked in dry blood. My heart sinks. "Well, Banks, we now know that they were definitely here. Now what?!"

Banks is deep in thought and doesn't immediately respond to my question. When he does, he chooses not to tell me about the other drops of blood that his experienced eyes noticed on the floor. We head back up the steps to the main level, and he pulls out his phone.

"Hey Marna, this is Banks," he says. "Clay and I are over at the old Stine cabin now. You and Perrin were right! That woman who rented the cabin is definitely involved with abducting the president and the boy. They were here, but now they're gone. I figure we missed them by only a few minutes. Do you and Perrin have any idea where they might be heading? I have a sinking feeling that we're running out of time before they get away for good."

I can't hear Marna's voice well, but Banks listens intently to her and waits for her to bring Perrin into the conversation.

"Mom, didn't Rini mention something about meeting some friends around Cornucopia?"

"Yeah, I remember that now, but she could've been making that up," Marna replies.

"Cornucopia, huh?" Banks says out loud. He ponders that and thinks about its remoteness and the fact that it's located on the shore of Lake Superior.

"Gotta go, ladies!" Banks says to Marna and Perrin. "I'll let you know if your intuition is as good about Cornucopia as it was about the Stine cabin."

"We're going to need a car," Banks says to me. "That pickup truck sure isn't going anywhere." He pulls his phone out again and places another telephone call to a man who knows Douglas and Bayfield counties as well as anyone.

Sheriff Muggs Larabee answers his cell phone on the second ring.

"Larabee here!"

"Muggs, it's Banks. I'm with Clay Arnold at the Stine property. We need your help, pronto!"

Banks gives the sheriff a sketchy description of what he and Clay found at the cabin and what Marna and Perrin shared with them.

"Muggs, bring an unmarked car," Banks advises. "I'll fill you in more when you get here."

"I'm on my way, Banks. Boy, I'd love to show up those feds."

Sheriff Larabee commandeers his deputy's 4Runner and turns north on Route 27 from Motts Ravine. He and Deputy Goldfine had been to the ravine investigating reports of suspicious behavior that the lieutenant informed him about. Muggs knew that it was just a ruse by the feds and General Swift to get him out of the way. Apparently, they didn't want some small-town yokel hanging around messing things up.

Muggs has been in law enforcement in Douglas County for some thirty years now. He'd risen through the ranks of the department and became sheriff ten years ago. He runs a tight ship with very modest financial resources and manages to hire and retain good men and women, all eight of them. But there's one man who's judgment and experience he's learned to trust above all others, Banks. He doesn't know everything about Banks's background, but he knows enough from his own experiences with the man to come running if Banks calls and says he needs some help.

Banks and I are waiting outside the Stine cabin when Sheriff Larabee pulls up to us. We climb inside the 4Runner. Banks takes the front passenger seat, and I'm barely situated in the back seat when the sheriff throws the vehicle into drive and sprays gravel and sand with his tires as he makes for the highway.

"Where too, Banks?!" he shouts above the road noise.

"Cornucopia, Muggs! We have a hunch that's where they're taking the president and Bodie."

"How'd you come up with your hunch?" Muggs asks.

"Marna and Perrin," Banks replies.

"Oh really," Muggs guffaws. "I wasn't aware we had a mother-and-daughter investigative firm in the town of Brule," he deadpans.

"You can laugh, sheriff," I say from the back seat, "but they've given us better leads than the entire military and security people have."

"Point taken, Mr. Arnold!"

In a few minutes they approach the junction of County Road B and Route 27. "Wait a minute," Muggs says. "Something doesn't look right."

He had deployed two officers to create a roadblock at this junction earlier, but he didn't spot his men. All he saw was the flashing lights of the cruiser illuminating the surrounding fir trees.

"We've got to stop here a minute. I need to check on my men."

Muggs sees Banks glance at his watch and says, "Don't worry, Banks, but I've got to check on these guys first."

Both of us get out of the 4Runner with the sheriff, and he goes directly over to the cruiser and turns off the flashing lights. I go over to the side of the road to pee and see the lifeless eyes of one of the deputies staring into the night sky from the ditch below. It's a heartbreaking scene.

"Over here," I shout, and the sheriff comes trotting over.

"Oh no," he moans. "No, no."

He slides down into the ditch near his fallen deputy and closes his officer's lifeless eyes. He radios Deputy Goldfine, "You better get up here to the junction."

His next sentence is interrupted by Banks shouting from across the road, "Here's the other officer."

"Hurry up, Goldfine. We've got to get to Cornucopia. I need you to get up here ASAP and secure this scene and retrieve their bodies. Call the EMS team and whatever backup you think you need. I'll go see their wives when I get back."

They disconnect their call, and we climb back into the 4Runner. The look on Muggs Larabee's face matches the expressions that Banks and I have been wearing ever since Bodie and the president got abducted. All three of us are pissed-off, worried, and determined to get them back ... safely.

Chapter 28

RINI DRIVES THE SUV within the legal speed limit as she approaches the town of Brule. Every few seconds she casts a glance to her rearview mirror to see if they're being followed. It's a little after 11:30 PM now, and most folks in Douglas County are snug in their beds, leaving Rini to believe that anyone out at this hour is likely to be a member of law enforcement or the military.

The town of Brule is tiny, and it takes Rini no time to stop at the intersection of Route 27 and Route 2, but instead of turning east on Route 2 toward Ashland, she drives north on County Road H. She knows the county road will be even

less traveled plus its the most direct route to State Route 13. She has Alexei confirm on his map that this route will take them along the Lake Superior coast to their ship anchored in Siskiwit Bay near the town of Cornucopia. No one speaks inside the vehicle. Each occupant feels anxious, but with each passing mile, they begin to relax slightly sensing that they are about to pull off the greatest subterfuge in modern Russian history, the abduction of the President of the United States of America.

They cruise through the sleepy hamlet of Waino, and about a mile later they merge onto State Route 13.

"We are getting closer. Another thirty minutes and we'll be in Cornucopia," Rini says. "Stay sharp and be sure you keep a watchful eye on our passengers, Viktor!"

After giving Deputy Goldfine his instructions to retrieve the officers' bodies from the highway, Sheriff Larabee floors the 4Runner and speeds north toward Lake Superior. He thinks about calling the sheriff in Bayfield County to render assistance, but he and Banks agree that having the cavalry arrive in Cornucopia before we get there could jeopardize everything. Sitting in the back seat I feel my phone vibrate, and I see that it's Maggie calling.

"Hi honey," I say. "I wish I had good news to share with you about Bodie, but we're still searching. Banks and I did find where the Russians had been holding him and the president, but they'd left by the time we got there."

To her credit, Maggie is managing to keep it together, but I can tell from the softness of her voice that she is consumed by fear for our little boy.

"Right now Banks and I are in a car being driven by Sheriff Larabee, and we think we know where they're taking them. I know how hard this is for you, and I wish I had more positive news to share, but I promise to call you the minute we get Bodie back."

We speak for a few moments longer, and I tell her I love her, but that I need to hang up. I just can't bear hearing the sadness in her voice without having positive information that would assuage her fear.

Banks looks over his shoulder at me and says, "We'll get them back, Clay."

I wish I could feel as convinced as he's trying to make me feel. I nod my head at him appreciatively, but both he and I know that this may not end well at all.

Muggs Larabee speeds through the intersection at Brule and chews up pavement as he zooms through the town of Waino. I stare out my window vacantly and feel totally helpless to save my son. I touch the handgun in my lap and the Demon camera in my pocket. In all of my years as an avenging vigilante, I've never wanted to use a lethal weapon on someone as much as I do right now. The trees and houses go by us in a blur, but the three of us are focused on one goal, and we're getting closer with each mile that passes. I look at the 4Runner's speedometer. It shows eighty-two miles per hour. I wish we could go even faster.

Some fifteen miles ahead on State Route 13 Rini obeys the posted speed limits as she drives through the towns of Port Wing and Herbster.

"What is a herbster?" Alexei asks aloud. "Is that the little furry animal that runs around in a wheel in a cage?"

Rini looks at her agent in the passenger's seat as if he's had a stroke. "That's a hamster, you idiot, and keep your mind on the mission. We should arrive at Cornucopia shortly." And true to her word they see a sign indicating the town is two miles ahead.

"Check on our passengers, Viktor, are they still unconscious?"

"Yes, Rini, they're still asleep but probably not for much longer."

Unbeknown to them, though, Jake Horvath has begun waking up. He lies stone still beneath the tarpaulin listening to their words and the sound of the tires on the road. The effects of the sedative are dissipating, but he still feels their unsettling influence. He senses that he is not alone under the tarp and intuits that it's Bodie's unconscious body next to him.

"We're here," Rini announces. "Now we need to find the pier next to Fullerton's Fisheries and our comrade, Mikhail Borodin."

She drives slowly through the center of town which is deathly quiet as the town hall's clock strikes midnight. She crosses the bridge over the Siskiwit River and immediately sees Fullerton's Fisheries on her left and the long pier leading out into the darkness of Siskiwit Bay and Lake Superior beyond. A large, dark ship looms in front of them at the end of the pier.

"We're here!" she announces triumphantly. "We've made it!"

She drives to the end of the pier and turns off her headlights. Mikhail Borodin steps out of the shadows and directs them where to park. He has a broad smile on his face as he approaches the car.

"Irina!" Mikhail gushes. "You and your men are true heroes for Mother Russia! Let's see the prize you have brought us."

Irina, Alexei, and Viktor exit the car and each is embraced by Mikhail. "Let's hurry now," Mikhail exhorts them. "We set sail as soon as we have our, uh, cargo on board."

Jake and Bodie are still under the tarpaulin, and Bodie has begun to regain consciousness too. Jake feels him begin to move and quietly cautions him to remain still. Bodie resists at first as he tries to regain his full faculties, but then he hears Russian being spoken, and he heeds the president's advice.

Suddenly a beam from a car's headlight flashes on Fullerton's Fisheries, and a local patrol car pulls onto the pier and heads toward the ship. The four Russians stand frozen in the police car's headlight, and Rini moves in its direction to speak with the policeman. Viktor and Alexei instinctively touch the pistols in their pockets and wait to see what unfolds. Mikhail recedes into the shadows again.

"Evening folks," Officer Neville Tweedie says evenly. "It's a little late to being hanging out on Fullerton's dock, don't you think?"

"Yes it is, officer," Rini confirms brightly. "Our ship is preparing to leave. We're late departing because we were waiting for a final shipment to be delivered. It's here now though. I hope we haven't disturbed anyone."

Officer Tweedie exits his cruiser and walks over to the SUV. "And what do you have being delivered at this hour?" he inquires, and just as he's about to inspect the interior of Rini's car, he hears a large thumping sound and muffled shouts coming from the car's rear cargo area.

"What the …?!" the officer exclaims. "Who's back there?"

He walks to the rear of the Highlander and begins to open the rear door when Alexei and Viktor grab him firmly and throw him to the ground. The officer tries to grab his service revolver when the silenced sound of Alexei's Makarov ends the policeman's existence as a sentient being on planet Earth.

"Quickly, before anyone else comes. We must get rid of him," Rini insists.

Viktor and Alexei pick up the dead peace officer and place his slumped body into the rear of his cruiser. They put the car in neutral and release the cruiser's parking brake. Both men push the cruiser to the edge of the pier and with one final strong shove, they send it cascading into the deep water at the end of the dock. The splash is loud, but at this hour no one is the wiser. The police cruiser floats briefly and then succumbs to gravity as it sinks to the bottom of Siskiwit Bay.

The three Russians look nervously about, hoping that no one else has witnessed the drama. Mikhail returns from the shadows and exhales his relief.

"That was too close," he states the obvious. "Let's move. We cannot afford any further confrontations, especially now that the president and the boy are awake."

Rini instructs Alexei to prepare the dart gun with more sedative, and they gather at the rear of the SUV. The shouts from inside the car grow louder, and Viktor opens the rear door and points his pistol at the bleary-eyed boy and the enraged leader of the free world.

"If you think for one minute that you'll ever get me to Russia alive, think again!" Jake shouts, and he savagely kicks his foot into Viktor's face which is already grossly disfigured from removing Bodie's fish hooks. The Russian yelps in pain, and Alexei prepares to discharge the dart gun. Mikhail motions for Alexei to wait.

"A noble effort, Mr. President," Mikhail offers, "but one more move like that and the boy is dead, yes?!"

Viktor regains his footing and grabs Jake. He pulls him out of the vehicle and onto the pavement while Alexei awaits instructions from Rini and her boss.

Mikhail Borodin stands over him and gives Jake a haughty smirk.

"So, President Horvath, the so-called leader of the free world, I believe your capture proves that our Russian subterfuge trumps your Yankee ingenuity, eh?!"

"I wouldn't count on it, mister," Jake replies confidently. "And I promise you that if anything bad happens to my young friend here, I will personally execute you."

Mikhail smiles nervously. Rini tells Viktor to get Bodie out of the car and to bind the boy's ankles and wrists with duct tape which he does roughly.

"Throw him in the bay if the president misbehaves again," Rini commands. "No more disruptions. Let's get the president on board. Leave the boy for now. He's not going anywhere."

Jake begins to struggle again but abruptly stops when he sees Viktor put his gun to Bodie's temple.

Chapter 29

SHERIFF MUGGS LARABEE is driving like a man on fire. The president being abducted from the Brule River in his county is something that is just stuck in his craw. And, the thought of all these high-ranking officials coming into his jurisdiction and taking over is simply damn annoying. He focuses on the road ahead and races through the coastal town of Port Wing seeing nary a light. He accelerates even more and shortly thereafter the town of Herbster is in his rearview mirror.

Muggs slows the 4Runner as he enters the quaint town of Cornucopia, population ninety-eight people.

He asks, "Clay, did Marna or Perrin say where the Russians might be going here?"

"No, they didn't mention any place in particular, but my guess is that they'll use a ship again like they did with the *Svetlana* in Superior. That's just a hunch, but I vote we look for a pier large enough to dock a decent-sized ship." Banks nods his agreement.

"That would be Fullerton's Fisheries," Muggs states. "It's only three blocks away." He turns left and heads in that direction.

"Cut your lights, Muggs," Banks advises. Muggs complies, and a minute later we enter the large dock area very quietly.

"There!" Banks exclaims as he points to a dark ship docked at the deep end of the pier about seventy yards away. "I bet that's our target."

I can't begin to say how much I just want to bolt out of this car, run to that ship, and try to save my boy. I've struggled not to think about it too much, but seeing that dried blood on Bodie's handkerchief in the cabin has haunted me. I definitely don't want the president to be hurt, but Bodie's my son.

Muggs drives us forward very slowly on the pier, and we see a small cluster of people congregating between an SUV and the ship. Two of the individuals are lying on the ground. One looks like a larger person than the other.

"I think this is it!" Muggs advises. "I'm calling for backup, but in a faraway town like this, we may not get much support. I'm also calling General Swift. We definitely could use those rangers now!"

"That's fine," Banks says. "Are you ready, Clay? Let's go get our men."

"Damn right!" I say. "You lead the way!"

Banks and I exit the car. Each of us is holding a pistol behind our back. Our clips are full, and the safeties are off. We walk forward. Muggs radios for backup and follows us several seconds later.

"Good evening," a female's voice calls out. "Can we help you gentlemen with something?" Irina Nefsky asks politely.

Banks and I notice two of her companions slowly back up into the deep shadows of shipping containers stored on the dock. We look at each other and nod. We know that we're going to have to deal with them.

"Sure thing, ma'am," Sheriff Larabee replies. "You can help us by backing away from those two individuals that you're holding against their will. That would be a good start, and then we'll discuss what comes next."

"Now why would we want to do that when we hold all of the, uh, cards?" Mikhail Borodin responds.

"Banks! Is that you?" Jake Horvath asks loudly. "About time you figured out where we are. Hell, I thought Bodie and I would have to take these bastards apart all by ourselves."

At the mention of Bodie's name, I recognize for certain that he's the smaller figure lying on the ground.

"Bodie!" I shout. "Are you okay, son?"

"Dad!?! You're here?!"

"We've come to take you and Jake back home, Bodie."

"They're mean people, Dad. They cut the president's pinky finger off, and he got a wound in his side when they shot a gun in that room."

"I know, son," I say sympathetically. "It's all been really scary, but you're being very brave."

I start to walk in his direction when I see the older Russian man pull a pistol from his waist and shake his head no.

Banks holds me by my sleeve. "Let's take it slow, Clay," he says.

"Here's how it is going to be," Mikhail announces to the three of us. "We are going to load the president onto the boat. You can have the boy, and we will leave. Very simple. As in many negotiations both parties have to give up a little to gain what they want, yes?"

He walks over to President Horvath and puts his gun to his head. "Or perhaps you prefer that the boy dies instead," and he pivots and points the gun at Bodie.

It's everything I can do to not charge the bastard threatening my son. Banks holds me back again. Like ghosts in the night, Alexei and Viktor reappear and are standing in places flanking our position. We could easily be caught in a crossfire.

"You keep that guy on your right covered, okay Clay?"

I turn that way with my gun trained on the Russian when I hear a gun discharge. From twenty yards away Banks has put a single shot into his target's chest. Alexei Pulasky drops like a sack of cabbages, and everyone dives for cover as all hell breaks loose.

Mikhail and Rini run for protection behind the SUV while Viktor unleashes a torrent of shots at Banks and me. The heavy metal shipping containers we dive behind deflect his barrage. I note that the only people still out in the open are Jake and Bodie.

Jake stands, and it's obvious from his posture that he's withstood some real abuse at the hands of these criminals. Jake bends down near Bodie and tries to pick him up, but with his injured hand and side and Bodie's bound wrists and ankles, it's very awkward for him to do. He begins to drag Bodie off to the side out of harm's way when Rini charges forward. I fire a shot at her that just misses, and she slinks behind protective cover again. Mikhail and Rini both know that their opportunity for greatness is beginning to slip away. They've already lost one man, and this small-town sheriff has undoubtedly called for backup.

"Surely we can come to an agreement," Mikhail shouts but his voice isn't quite as convincing as it was a few minutes ago. All of a sudden a burst of weapons fire comes at us from the deck of the ship.

Mikhail laughs, "You didn't actually think we would sail this ship by ourselves did you?"

Banks, Muggs, and I stay close to our cover, and Jake continues to drag Bodie out of harm's way near the edge of the dock. It's amazing to me that neither one of us has been shot in this fusillade of bullets.

"Give it up, comrade!" Muggs hollers at Mikhail. "We've got you pinned own, and we have backup on the way. And even if you did manage to get on that ship, you know there's no way you can escape."

Another barrage of bullets comes from the ship.

"You may be right, Sheriff, but we can at least do some very serious damage here."

Mikhail peeks around the SUV and fires a shot that strikes the president's thigh and sends him to the ground. Bodie sees Jake lying there and rolls over on top of him to help protect him. Rini fires her gun next, and the bullet hits the wooden dock by Bodie causing sharp splinters of wood to stab his shoulder. I hear my son yelp in pain and holler for Banks and Muggs to cover me as I leap forward running and shooting as I go. Bullets are flying around all of us like angry hornets. I reach Bodie and Jake and grab each of them by their collar and with strength I didn't know that I had, I manage to pull them behind a large wall. Both of them are bleeding, but not profusely.

I hug Bodie as closely as I can without hurting his injured shoulder. Tears flow out of my eyes with relief, but I know we're not out of danger yet.

"Stay down, son!" I say. "I'll cut those bindings off of you once the shooting stops. Mr. President, hang tough, sir, just a little bit longer. We've got the calvary on the way." Jake nods his head but is clearly in discomfort.

There's a brief lull in the action as each group tries to decide the next best course of action. Banks knows that they're going to need medical attention and calls General Swift to request a medical helicopter in addition to his rangers.

"The rangers and medics are on their way," Banks tells Muggs. "Let's keep these assholes pinned down until they arrive."

Rini looks at the place where Viktor is positioned and shouts to him in Russian. The Russian agent recedes back into the shadows, and the next thing we know he's sneaked around the shipping containers on the dock and reemerges from the shadows standing fifteen feet away with his Makarov pointing at us. He has an evil grin on his face, and he shouts his success back to Rini and Mikhail.

"So, Sheriff, it appears that we have another standoff, yes?" Mikhail shouts. "Like I said a little earlier, we take the president, and you get to keep the boy and his father."

In the distance we hear the wail of police sirens coming our way. Hopefully they'll be in time with the general's men not too far behind. All of the adversaries on the dock realize that there's precious little chance that the Russian agents can now actually abduct the president to Russia as they'd always planned. The major concern now is that the Russians and the men on the ship kill all of us in one final burst of Russian bravado.

I take a shot at Viktor, and he returns my fire hitting my handgun and sending it skittering out of reach. Bodie tries to grab it, and Viktor shoots again in his direction with the bullet flying past us.

"Stay down!" I shout to Bodie again as I slide back next to him and Jake. We're in an untenable position as Viktor begins to close in on us. Banks and Muggs do not have a clear shot. Jake, Bodie, and I are on our own, and Viktor realizes that he has the upper hand as he cautiously strides in our direction, his grin widening.

Bodie shifts his weight off of the president and grabs onto me with fear etched on his face.

"Kill them all!" Mikhail commands. "If we can't have the president, then nobody can," he hollers childishly.

Banks and Muggs open fire at Viktor, Rini, and Mikhail without any positive effect other than trying to buy some more time.

"I'll save the president for last," Viktor declares, "but first I want to kill this little boy piece of shit that hurt my face."

Bodie buries his face into my chest and slips his hand inside my vest pocket. He feels something oddly familiar that I had shown him a few days ago. He finds the power button, pulls the Demon camera out of my pocket, points it in Viktor's direction, and presses the antique camera's shutter release button. An angry bolt of cobalt blue electricity fires out of my trusty Demon and engulfs the hapless Russian where he stands. He twitches, shakes, shimmies, and falls to the ground in a fried heap.

Screams of surprise echo from all of us as the wails of the police sirens grow louder and rhythmic thumps from a military helicopter grow closer. Rini and Mikhail realize that their opportunity to kidnap or even kill the American president is virtually gone now. Mikhail knows that the Kremlin will never forgive his failure so he uncharacteristically attempts one final attack on us. He runs across the dock in our direction shouting Russian curses, and Banks takes aim and his marine training takes over. The sound of a single round screams through the otherwise tranquil Northern Wisconsin night and drops the veteran spy midstride. Rini sees her handler fall to the ground dead.

We hear shouts from the men on the ship and see it slowly pulling away from the dock hoping to escape in the fog of Lake Superior.

Irina Nefsky, a.k.a. Rini Neff, knows that their attempt at glory is finally over. She makes one last heroic attempt to exude the pride of her Russian homeland and stands defiantly in front of Muggs Larabee who has rushed to meet her head on while Banks runs to help Jake, Bodie, and me.

The sheriff and the Russian agent stare intently at each other. As the police backup from the towns of Bayfield and Ashland finally arrive, Muggs offers a closing remark to Rini, "I've got me a badge and a gun. Wattya wanna do?!"

She sees the ship attempting to pull away from the dock. It's highlighted in bright spotlights from the arriving military helicopters, and she drops her gun in resignation. The terrifying confrontation in Cornucopia is finally over, and she's the last Russian standing. Muggs secures her in handcuffs, and two arriving officers lead her away.

The relief and joy that I feel in our saving Bodie and the president is overwhelming. Bodie and I cling to each other with tears wetting both of our faces. I take the Demon camera from his small hand and return it to my pocket. Banks renders immediate first aid to Jake, and the medics arrive very quickly at our position with two stretchers, one for Jake and the other for Bodie.

Banks and I briefly talk with Muggs. He's got the scene under control here, and he radios General Swift to inform him of the outcome. Banks and I climb into the helicopter as the medics secure Bodie and Jake in their gurneys for the flight. A moment later the copter lifts off, and I see the sleepy town of Cornucopia, Wisconsin, recede from view as our pilot radios ahead and makes a beeline for the University of Minnesota's trauma hospital in Duluth.

Chapter 30

DURING THE FLIGHT the medics clean and dress the president's wounds and put him on an IV. The bullet from Mikhail's gun had passed through his thigh but would likely require surgery to repair tissue. Fortunately the femur bone was spared.

I call Maggie to let her know that we've gotten Bodie and the president back safely. It was the first conversation I was looking forward to having with her in nearly three days.

"We're in a helicopter right now heading for the hospital in Duluth. Bodie's generally okay, but he's taken some hard lumps too. Here, you can talk with him."

I hand the phone to Bodie who musters as much bravado as the weary and battered lad can. "Hi Mom, how are you?"

"How am I?!?" I hear her ask incredulously. "The question is how are you? Are you in much pain, sweetheart?"

"I'm a little sore, Mom, but Jake, I mean the president has been hurt worse. He was really brave, and he helped protect me, Mom."

The two of them talk for a few minutes longer, and I can see that our bodacious one is getting very sleepy.

"Honey, we're getting ready to land at the hospital's helipad, and Bodie needs some rest," I say to her. "I'll call you back once the doctors examine him, and we get him settled in a room. They'll want to keep him for observation at least overnight. Why don't you make arrangements to fly to Duluth, and I'll meet you at the airport, okay?"

She agrees, and we hang up.

"Your boy's quite a warrior, Clay," I hear Jake Horvath say to me. "He saved my life on more than one occasion these past couple of days."

"Oh, thank you, sir, I thought you were asleep. He's quite a lad, that's for sure. Maggie and I refer to him as 'the bodacious one'. I'm very sorry that either of you had to go through this."

"I want you to know how grateful I am to both of you for your bravery, Clay. Not only did you guys save me. You potentially saved the world from an ugly geopolitical conflagration."

"I'm just glad that you're safe and that I got my boy back, Jake."

I see Banks coming back to talk with the president, and I yield my seat to him and turn to go to the cockpit. Banks takes my seat and tells us that he's spoken at length with General Swift about how things played out after we left Cedar Island. He's sending orders throughout our defense system to scale down the threat level.

"Thanks for taking care of that, Banks. We don't need to start a nuclear holocaust over a pinky finger," Jake deadpans.

"Seriously, how're you holding up, Jake?" Banks asks.

"Well, old friend, aside from getting my little finger cut off, losing a bunch of skin from my side, getting shot in the thigh, and smacked around by some big Russian thugs, I think I'm hanging in there. What's the status with the Russians that attacked us?"

"We put all of the Russians down except for a woman who was the lead agent. She's a tough bird named Irina Nefsky. Vladimir Badunov would likely say he's never heard of her; that she must be a rogue actor. Who knows, facing the rest of her life in prison might persuade her to be more cooperative with our team. Everyone else is dead, and the sailors on the ship are in custody. We lost two of Sheriff Larabee's deputies to these people near Brule, and apparently another officer in Cornucopia is missing and presumed dead. Divers are going to search the waters near the pier in the morning."

"I'm just heartbroken, Banks, that these innocent people got killed because of me, not to mention Bodie here getting roughed up. I'm glad he's sleeping okay now. He sure earned it. I told his dad a minute ago that his son's a warrior. I swear the kid has the heart of a lion, Banks, not unlike you back in the day. Thanks for coming for us, seriously. I owe you, again."

Banks nods, gives him a brotherly smile, and says, "Anytime."

"When I recover from this escapade in a little while," Jake says, "there's a message for Mr. Badunov that I'd like you to help send, if you're willing of course."

"Let's get you healed first, and then we'll talk," Banks replies.

The pilot comes on the intercom announcing that the helicopter is preparing to land. Other medical personnel will be waiting as soon as we touch down. I come back to join Jake and Banks and strap myself in. I'm relieved to see Bodie sleeping so peacefully.

Jake Horvath looks at the three of us and says, "Banks, I think we may have to induct two more men into our private little 'Oorah Society'. What do you think?"

"I think oorah that, Mr. President," Banks declares. "That's a done deal."

The skids from the helicopter settle on the roof of the hospital and the pilot turns off the rotors. Medical personnel immediately open the doors and gently carry both the president and Bodie indoors. I follow and bend down and kiss the top of my son's head. Bodie looks over at Jake and sees the president giving him a positive thumbs up.

"I'll catch up with you later, Bodie. I think the docs want to get me patched up a bit."

Bodie smiles at him and nods his understanding, and the two patients are wheeled in different directions.

Banks and I know it'll be a couple of hours before we can see the two of them again, so we go to the hospital's cafeteria to have something to eat. It's well past 2:00 AM and the food offerings are a little scant, but hospitals are like cities that never sleep, and we're able to load up on some breakfast.

"So much for a leisurely trip on the Brule River," I say to Banks with a sorry attempt at humor. "I don't think Bodie or I will ever be able to canoe past Cedar Island again without thinking about this chapter in the history of the 'river of presidents'," I say.

"No doubt!" Banks replies. "I'll be glad when this is all over for good, and Cecil Johns and I can immerse ourselves again in the quiet of the Brule River Forest. No telling what a mess of the place General Swift and his men have left for us."

"Maybe someday down the road Bodie and I can return for the relaxing drift on the river that we'd originally planned."

"You're always welcome at Cedar Island," Banks replies. "Do you think Bodie will still be up for going to Camp Voyager for the summer. I think camp is scheduled to open in three or four days."

"I guess we'll just have to wait and see how he feels. Plus, I'm not sure how Maggie will feel about his being gone from home all summer after this experience. We'll see."

Banks takes another sip of hot coffee and says, "By the way, Clay, what exactly was that curious gizmo that Bodie took from your pocket during our melee with the Russians?"

"Oh that," I say. "That's a special weapon called the Demon camera that my friends back home put together for me for, uh, special occasions. They took some spare parts from old cameras in our antique camera museum and created quite a killer stun gun."

"I'll say," Banks said. "I gotta get me one of those!"

"Yeah well, I had told Bodie that I never wanted him to use it unless I gave him permission. Good thing he just took matters into his own hands or the bastards could've gotten away with their plan."

"Sometimes it's better to ask for forgiveness after the fact than to ask for permission before," Banks offers.

"I agree with you, Banks, but I wasn't quite ready for my nine-year-old son to fry somebody's ass. Thank goodness he did though."

An ER doctor named Riley Edberg finds us in the cafeteria and informs us that Bodie has been examined and is remarkably stable given all that he's been through.

"We removed those nasty wooden splinters from his shoulder and cleaned up several other cuts and abrasions. We want to keep him for a day or so though, as much to look for symptoms of post-traumatic stress as anything physical."

"Thanks Doc," I say. "When can I see him?"

"Give us a while to get him into his room on the med-surge floor. I think it's best if he just sleeps for a few hours. You can visit him briefly when we get him settled, but he definitely needs to rest."

"How's the president doing?" Banks asks.

"I assisted Dr. Amy Elliot with the surgery on his thigh. He'll probably need to use a cane for a while, but Dr. Elliot and I both think he should heal reasonably well. The flesh wound to his side should also heal fine over time, but unfortunately he'll only have a little nub of a pinky finger. Not much we can do about that. We've got a guest lounge with a couple of beds if you guys want to get some shuteye while we finish up with the patients."

Banks and I both nod our understanding and thank Dr. Edberg for keeping us informed. We've gone a long time now without sleep, and we take the doc up on the suggestion to rest up.

My phone rings, and it's Maggie calling me. "How's Bodie doing?" she asks.

I tell her the medical report Dr. Edberg has just given us, and she audibly calms down with the good news.

"I also just received a phone call from a General Swift," she says. "He's sending a military helicopter to pick me up at home and fly me to the hospital, so you don't have to worry about picking me up at the Duluth airport."

"That's good news, honey. I can't wait for you to get here, and for our little family to be together again. I hope all is well with Tori and Mace and our critters."

"Everyone will be so relieved about Bodie," she says. "I'll see you in a few hours, Clay. I love you, honey."

"Thanks Maggie, I love you too. I'm just so sorry this happened. I promise I'll keep a close eye on the bodacious one until you get here."

Chapter 31

THE NEXT FEW DAYS go by without any of the stress and trauma of the previous days. Once Jake Horvath recovers well enough from his injuries and surgery to travel, he returns to Washington to handle all things presidential. His main order of business is to calm any fears among our own people and our allies about his well-being, and to make certain all of our military personnel and missile systems are reduced to a lower state of readiness.

Banks returns to Cedar Island where he and Cecil Johns work to return their peaceful part of the world back to normalcy. All of the military and security people are long gone now from the Brule

River Forest, but these recent days of turmoil will forever be an unforgettable chapter in the legendary history of the "river of presidents."

Sheriff Larabee got his county back under control, but he has the very sad duty of speaking to the families of his two fallen officers and attending their funerals. Douglas County is a series of closely knit communities, and residents find some solace in knowing that Muggs and his men and women are on the job.

Irina Nefsky, a.k.a. Rini Neff, is currently housed in a special, high-security facility in Virginia awaiting trial for multiple offenses ranging from kidnapping and murder to operating as an unregistered foreign agent. She says she's willing to cooperate, but one never knows when it comes to good old Russian subterfuge. It's highly doubtful that she'll ever see the outside of a federal prison again.

As for Bodie, well, thank goodness for the resilience of youth. He was discharged from the hospital two days after being admitted through the emergency room. In reality his physical condition was such that he could've been discharged a day earlier, but Maggie insisted that the hospital keep him for another day. I don't think Maggie would've taken no for an answer. I worry about Bodie's emotional state after all that occurred and know that I want to have a heart-to-heart conversation with my son before too long.

Bodie, Maggie, and I leave the hospital and drive south from Duluth heading back to our motel room in Brule. We drive across the Bong bridge and enter the city of Superior, and before long we pass the exit for the Quebec Pier where the *Svetlana* had been anchored. I cast a long glance in that direction, expecting to still see the ship at anchor, but it has sailed on to parts unknown. Frankly, I see nothing to be gained by discussing the ship with Maggie and Bodie and telling them about finding the president's pinky finger there. Some things are just best left unspoken.

We arrive at the Grey Gables Motel in Brule and are greeted by Tillie at the front desk.

"Well, hello," she says as we enter. "I hadn't seen you for a couple of days and wondered if you had left without checking out."

"Sorry about that," I say to Tillie. "We've been a little preoccupied with other things," I admit matter-of-factly.

"Wow! I guess you could say the same for all of us around here," she adds. "You heard about all of the commotion that went on with the Russians and the president, didn't you?"

"Yeah," Bodie says. "That must've been pretty scary, huh?"

I tell Tillie that I'll let her know in a bit how long we'll be staying. I also need to make arrangements to drop off the rental car we were given, courtesy of Uncle Sam, and pick up my Tacoma at the Winneboujou canoe landing where Gus transported us to Stone's Bridge and the beginning of our Brule River adventure.

"I'm hungry," Bodie states as we enter our motel room. "Do you think we can go back to Marna's Place for lunch? Mom, you'll really like their mooseburgers," he laughs.

"Well, darling, mooseburgers sure wouldn't be my first choice, but if that's what you want, I think I can pretend they're made out of soy or something healthful."

I'm happy merely to listen to their playful banter and feel relieved that the bodacious one still has a sense of humor.

We leave the motel and drive to pick up my truck at the Winneboujou landing and then head for Marna's Place. The car agency will pick up the rental car later. As we enter the diner, I see the same old geezers, Bertram and Fred, sitting in the same booth as before. They're both too engrossed in their newspapers to look up.

"My goodness!" Marna exclaims as we select a booth. "It's our national heroes!"

I introduce Maggie to Marna and Sarah too as she rushes out from the kitchen to greet us. I explain to Maggie that it was Marna and her other daughter, Perrin, who were the keys to our finding Bodie and the president. Maggie stands up and hugs both of them warmly.

"I can't thank you enough for everything you did to help save our son," Maggie says tearfully. "You're the real heroes as far as I'm concerned, and we'll be forever in your debt."

"Yup!" comes an unsolicited chirp of affirmation from Bertram at the booth by the door.

Marna takes our lunch orders, which did not include any meaty mooseburgers, and the three of us settle in as a family again.

"Well, Bodie," Maggie begins, "are you ready to come home?"

The bodacious one looks over at me questioningly and says, "But, but I still want to go to Camp Voyager. Dad says the season begins tomorrow, and I thought that camp looked really fun when we visited there before our Brule River trip."

Maggie glances at me with a concerned look on her face. "You've been through an awful lot, Bodie, are you sure you don't want to come home and spend the summer with us, and Mace, Tori, Satchmo, and Lex? Rennie'll be home from college soon too."

Bodie looks at me for guidance, and I say, "It's your call, son."

"How about we do this," Bodie replies. "I'd really like to be a Little Dipper in the same cabin Dad was. Maybe you can all come up for parents' weekend in a few weeks?"

I smile at our son's mature suggestion and give him a private, fatherly wink.

"Can you live with that, Maggie?" I ask. "He's right about Camp Voyager being a lot of fun, and I know that Bern Lorber and the staff will help keep a close eye on our guy."

Maggie nods her head reluctantly and says, "Okay Mister Bodie, but only if you still promise to write me a couple of times a week!"

"Deal!" Bodie replies, "and this time it's Fred at the other booth who says, "Yup!" as he absently turns a page in his newspaper.

After lunch the three of us say goodbye to Marna and Sarah and head back to the Grey Gables for a much-earned nap and to organize our gear. I call Tillie at the front desk to let her know that we'll be checking out in the morning.

While Maggie and Bodie go over his belongings, I walk out to the Tacoma to stow my camera equipment. I also take a few minutes to call Bern Lorber to confirm that we'll be dropping Bodie off in the morning.

"He's been through a lot, Bern, but I can't think of a much better place for a kid to forget a tragic episode than the nurturing environs of camp. Plus, it's what Bodie really wants to do."

I share with Bern several details about what happened with the Russians that the media never knew about, and he understands our concerns totally. He promises to try to assuage any apprehension Maggie has when we meet at camp tomorrow morning. In my heart I know that Bodie's spending the summer at Camp Voyager is a good thing to do.

So, Maggie, Bodie, and I agree that we'll drop the bodacious one off at camp and spend some time there so Maggie can grow more comfortable with the idea. Then Maggie and I will take two days to drive the eleven hours back home to Indiana, and four weeks later we'll fly back to Duluth and visit Bodie at camp for parents' weekend.

Chapter 32

MID-JUNE IN MOSCOW, Russia is quite lovely. The snow has abated, bright flowers are in bloom, and the dour looks of many of its people are replaced by warm smiles of hope. Muscovites and tourists alike stroll along the Moskva River, amble past St. Basil's Cathedral, and saunter through Red Square.

Today, Chris Helton is one such tourist, at least that's what he wants the Russian security forces to believe. He's an American who's traveled to Moscow on business numerous times over the years, and he's developed helpful relationships with several Russian entrepreneurs during his visits. Some of

those Russian business people aren't exactly in love with the Kremlin but wisely manage to stay below the radar with their dissenting views. To do otherwise would be a death sentence.

In addition to being a tourist, Chris Helton is also a retired marine with a highly specialized skill. With his sniper's rifle he can shoot the center of a target five hundred yards away. He developed this skill by regular practice and by taking out bad guys during two tours of duty in Iraq and Afghanistan. Back in those days he also served alongside two other marines, Jake Horvath and Banks. These three men trust and know each other very well. They've kept in touch.

Chris walks through Red Square and sees the Moscow Kremlin looming in front of him. It's a fortified complex at the heart of Moscow and is the best known of the Russian citadels. It has five palaces, four cathedrals, and the enclosing Kremlin Wall. The complex also serves as the official residence of the President of the Russian Federation, Vladimir Badunov.

Chris carries a dark satchel and enters a building opposite the Kremlin that one of his friendly Russian contacts owns. He climbs a couple of flights of stairs, takes a key that was given to him and enters a small office with a window overlooking the Kremlin. He makes a call on an untraceable phone and waits to hear a familiar voice.

An aide knocks on the huge, gilded door leading to the presidential residence. He waits a moment, and a shirtless Badunov answers his knock.

"Yes, what is it, Yuri?" Badunov asks.

"There's an important call for you, sir, from the Americans."

"Oh, what is it they want now? I suppose they're still annoyed because of that, uh, episode, in that place called Wisconsin." He laughs. "I told them that I don't know anything about it, but they seem to think otherwise. Just take a message and tell them I'll get back to them, Yuri."

"Uh sir, it is the President of the United States himself. He says he'll hold for you."

"Oh. Very well, Yuri, transfer the call to my bedroom, and I'll speak with him from there."

Badunov closes the door and returns to his stately bedroom. He walks to his desk, picks up his phone, and strides over to the windows overlooking the walled enclosure of the Moscow Kremlin. He stands in front of a large picture window and prepares to be lectured by Jacob Horvath.

His phone rings and he answers the call with his customary reptilian detachment.

"Dah, hello. Is this Jacob?" Badunov asks evenly. "Hello, Mr. President?"

"Yes, I'm on the line, Mr. Badunov. Let's get to the point. You and your people kidnapped me, physically attacked me, hurt a boy, killed innocent people, put the whole friggin' world in nuclear peril. For what?"

"Oh, Mr. President, surely you don't think I would call for such action, especially against an important man like yourself. I'm told that the perpetrators were Russian, yes, but that they were rogue agents. I send you my sympathies, although while we are being direct, Mr. President, perhaps I can tell you that sanctions that you and your predecessors have placed on my country in recent years have rendered us as a second-rate nation in the eyes of the world. That is something I cannot tolerate, so perhaps these rogue agents weren't really rogue after all. In any event what are you going to do about it?"

The American government's private communications satellites orbit miles overhead and coordinate calls between Washington, DC, Cedar Island, and Moscow. Banks and Chris Helton listen to Jake Horvath's conversation with the Russian leader.

"Well, Badunov, if you think those earlier sanctions were painful, then hold on to something tight because financially they're about to get much worse, and I will do likewise to any country that chooses to continue to do business with you. And, if you want to threaten our friends in Europe with ceasing oil shipments to them, I can assure you that our increase in pumping has us in a position to fill their needs. You and I both know that America can easily outlast you. And for what, Vladimir? Because you're embarrassed that your system of government is a failure? That you can't compete economically with other nations? So you choose to act like a petulant child and throw a temper tantrum. You're a poor excuse for a leader, Badunov."

"Okay, Mr. Big Shot President, I've listened long enough. I'm a busy man. What do you want to do?"

"Just this!" he says vaguely. "Take it now, Chris."

The sound of the .408 Cheyenne Tactical round shattering the window's glass is followed by a banshee-like wail coming from Vladimir Badunov's mouth. Chis Helton watches him closely through his telescopic sight and sees the Russian's hand holding the phone get blown away by the bullet. The call ends.

"Banks, Chris, are you guys still on the line?" Jake asks. "How'd we do?"

"Mission accomplished," Chris says. "but I better scoot right quick now before Vladimir's minions show up!"

"Banks, we'll talk soon," Jake says. "I just wanted that son of a bitch to know that if he comes for a finger, I'm taking his goddamn hand."

"Oorah that, Jake. We'll talk soon!"

Chapter 33

THE WEEKS LEADING TO mid-July pass painstakingly slowly for both Maggie and me. We're certainly busy with our careers and helping to keep the brewery complex in order, but we miss our son. True to his word Bodie writes to us at least twice a week from Camp Voyager, and it's clear from his letters that he's made some good buddies and is enjoying a lot of his camping activities. Periodically, Maggie and I call the camp director, Bern Lorber, to get his read on Bodie.

"His counselor and I have both kept a watchful eye on him, and we've purposefully not said much to any others about what he experienced before the

camp season began. He seems to be fitting in quite well actually."

The only camp activity that Bodie was reluctant to do was canoe the Brule River with his cabin mates, but he faced his demons and had a good time. I understand the only sore point of their canoe trip was when they approached Cedar Island, and Larry Erikson teased Bodie for boasting that he'd met the President of the United States there.

"Yeah, and I'm Paul Bunyan," Larry had chided. "There's no way you ever met the president."

Bodie just let the whole discussion go, and he promised himself he wouldn't bring the subject up again.

Finally, parents' weekend arrives, and Maggie and I fly to Duluth and rent a car. Maggie's demeanor is what you'd expect of a loving mother who hasn't seen her child in several weeks. She's excited beyond words. I, on the other hand, am a little distracted by being back in a part of the world that just a few weeks earlier had things happen that terrified me to my core. I mean, I love the area, but …"

As Maggie and I drive through the city of Superior, I again cast a long glance at the road leading to the Quebec Pier where the *Svetlana* had been docked. I choose to keep things positive and not say a word to Maggie about Banks and me finding Jake Horvath's little finger there. We drive on

US Route 53 past Amnicon Falls and merge onto Route 2 heading East. Along the way we go through the familiar towns of Poplar, Maple, Blueberry, and Bellwood eventually arriving at the entrance to Camp Voyager on Lake Winneboujou.

As Maggie and I get out of our car, and I see the sign for camp and the Big House beyond, my mood lightens, and I begin to feel that I am again back on hallowed ground. We enter the Big House, and Bern Lorber greets us warmly.

"Maggie, Clay, welcome!" Bern says. "I'm so glad you were able to make it for parents' weekend. We've got a room fixed up for you in the Big House, and I'm glad you'll be staying for our Sunday evening campfire tonight. We have a number of other parents here as well, plus I understand we might have some special guests too."

Bern has one of his staff help stow our gear in our room, and we ask Bern where Bodie might be now.

"He should be on the waterfront with the rest of his village. The Little Dippers are preparing for a swim meet against our friendly arch rivals at Camp Nebagamon. Why don't you walk on down there and see him? We'll be having dinner before too long, and then we'll have our camp family campfire afterward."

Maggie and I stroll through camp, and I'm happy to see that she has a broad smile on her face.

"Clay, I can easily understand why a place like Camp Voyager can have such a positive impact on a kid," she says.

We approach the waterfront and see that boys and camp staff are all over the place swimming, canoeing, sailing, motorboating, and fishing. The shouts of excitement echo from the sheds and carry across the lake. We look for Bodie but don't see him at first. Then, we see his laughing face in the water as he touches the dock in a swim race that he's just won.

"Let's just watch for a second, Maggie," I say, and we're rewarded by seeing the other boys congregating around our son as they celebrate his victory.

"C'mon!" I exhort to Maggie, and we walk the rest of the way down to the swimming dock.

Bodie looks up and sees us standing on the dock smiling down at him, and the bodacious one darn near loses his swimming trunks as he clambers out of the lake to give us both wet hugs.

"Mom, Dad, you made it! I'm so glad you're here. I've got so much to show and tell you."

"Of course, we made it," I say to my son. "You didn't honestly think I was going to let you eat all of those mooseburgers by yourself," I tease.

Thankfully, Bodie thinks my snarky comment is pretty funny because Maggie shoots me a look that implies that I'm one weird dude. Oh well.

After showing Maggie and me his cabin and introducing us to his counselor and bunkmates, Maggie and I join the camp family in the dining hall for Sunday supper. Despite the clatter of dishes and the cacophony from young boys' voices, Maggie is thrilled by the camaraderie and enthralled by Camp Voyager's ninety-year history graphically displayed by plaques, photographs, and signs covering virtually every inch of interior wall space. Finally, she has a real sense of the magic of Camp Voyager.

I can't begin to adequately say how relieved I am by that, but even more I'm just so damn grateful to have the three of us together with a wonderful home and friends to return to. I think of my now deceased friend, Weed Rawlins, and how much he would appreciate this moment. Somehow I managed to save the handkerchief that was originally his that Bodie wrapped the president's wounded hand with. It's the little things that help connect and anchor us, I muse to myself. Anyway …

After supper Bern Lorber stands at the campy podium and welcomes the parents who are visiting and gives a few quick announcements.

"We'll be starting our Sunday evening campfire shortly. Counselors, please make sure your guys use the Jop before coming to the council circle. Oh, and I understand that we may be having a few special guests joining us this evening as well, so let's make sure everyone receives a great Camp Voyager welcome. See you in fifteen!"

Naturally, I had to avail myself to the Jop. Great, quirky little building. As I exit it, I look left and see my old cabin, Little Dipper One, now Bodie's home for the summer. Taking in this scene and having the moments we're all enjoying now, I shake my head in wonder that I ever had a career as an avenging vigilante. But, I did, and I'm okay with that, just as I'm okay with wanting to leave the violence behind me now. But what this terrifying experience on the Brule River reinforced in me is this: Don't ever come after a member of my family or someone in my inner circle. We all have our demons, and I keep my Demon camera close at hand in my jacket pocket.

Maggie, Bodie, and I arrive at the great council ring. As we enter we're each given a short key log which will be used at the conclusion of the ceremony. The council ring is set up like an amphitheater with four rows of wooden benches. As guests we're directed to take a seat in front. Finally, all 240 campers and the camp staff file in and take their seats.

Bern stands off to the side as he begins to talk. He speaks about personal goals and friendships made, of skills learned and those yet to be mastered. He speaks about the nature around us and the need to be caring stewards. And then, as he often does at the council fires, Bern recites his favorite poem by Edwin Markham: *"There is a destiny which makes us brothers; none goes his way alone. All that we send into the lives of others comes back into our own."*

From the treetops we see a flock of roosting crows suddenly take flight, and a few moments later we hear a rhythmic thumping sound, and the lights from a large helicopter illuminate the upper ball diamond. A minute later the guests that Bern Lorber had alluded to during supper appear. A hush eventually falls on the camp family as President Jacob Horvath appears with his friends Banks, Sheriff Muggs Larabee, and Marna, Sarah, and Perrin Philips.

Bern warmly welcomes all and directs them to benches in front that he's reserved for them. He briefly returns to the podium.

"I know. I know. You're probably thinking that if I can bring the President of the United States to Camp Voyager halfway through our season, what could I possibly do at the conclusion of the summer, right?!"

Friendly laughs and one or two shouts are voiced.

"Seriously though, everybody, President Horvath and his friends have asked to join us for a special presentation." Bern turns to Jake Horvath, yields the podium, and says," Sir, you honor us."

Jake Horvath stands and walks to the podium. His leg is about 80 percent recovered from the gunshot, and he strides with confidence but with a little discomfort. Bodie can't believe he's seeing Jake again, and I must admit that Maggie and I are more than a little in awe of the situation as well. Banks and I catch each other's eye and give nods and smiles of appreciation.

"Thank you very much, Mr. Lorber, for allowing my friends and I to descend on your fine evening. Honestly folks, I'm really quite fortunate to be here at all. As many of you know I was involved in an altercation right here in Douglas County about a month ago with some rather unpleasant foreign agents. I'm not the sort of fellow to forget people when they do something very helpful, and I've let these folks who are with me know how grateful I am. Jake turns and looks at Banks and at each of them again and smiles warmly.

There's a couple of other folks that I never got a chance to properly thank when all of this hulla-baloo occurred. Without them, I wouldn't be here today. Clay and Bodie Arnold, would you please step forward and join me?"

Bodie looks at me with a confused smile on his face, and despite all of the accolades that I've received throughout my photographic career, I'm confused as well about what's coming next.

Banks steps forward and stands next to his old friend, Jake, holding two shallow, decorative boxes. Jake embraces me and then kneels down on one knee and gives Bodie a friendly, paternal hug.

"I didn't really get a chance to say goodbye to you, Jake," Bodie exclaims.

"I know, my friend, that's why I'm here now."

Jake stands again, looks over at Banks and nods his head. Banks opens the first box, and from its red velvet lining, he lifts out a shiny medallion on a blue ribbon. Jake pins the medal to my shirt over my heart. Banks then hands him the contents of the second box, and the president pins the same medal to Bodie's shirt. He places his hands on Bodie's and my shoulders.

"When I was a younger man, I was a marine. I thought that serving my country in battle was the greatest sacrifice that a person could make. I still believe that, but I've come to realize that there are many different types of battles to be waged, and that warfare is only one. Clay, your perseverance and fortitude helped save my life, and indeed the world from calamitous retaliations. Please accept my personal thanks and that of a grateful nation."

"Bodie, my friend, we sure went through a lot together. You were there for me in my times of need like very few people have ever been, and we made it. You're a hero in my eyes."

Bodie is beaming with bewilderment. Maggie is wiping tears of joy from her cheeks, I'm grinning like a baboon, and everyone at the council fire is spellbound by what's happening. Poor Larry Erikson, Bodie's cabinmate, is totally chagrined that Bodie was telling the truth about meeting the president.

"It is for these reasons," Jake continues, "that I am proud to confer on both of you the Presidential Medal of Freedom which is the highest civilian honor our country can give."

At the conclusion of his presentation, everyone in camp goes nuts with pure elation. Maggie comes running to join the three of us, and Banks saunters over to greet us as well. As the campers and staff file out, they toss their key logs onto the campfire until there is a large, warm blaze illuminating the council ring.

"Thanks again, Bodie! For all you did," Jake says as Maggie and I look proudly on. "And remember, Bodie, you and your folks are always welcome at the White House."

"Really!" Bodie exclaims.

Jake nods his head affirmatively at the bodacious one, holds up his disfigured left hand, and with a grin says, "Pinky swear!"

~ The End ~

About the Author

Stuart Fabe

OVER THE LAST FOUR DECADES, Stuart Fabe has directed his creative energies to three artistic media: photography, weaving, and writing. He has published several books showcasing his fine-art photography and his intricate weavings. He has exhibited artwork at numerous art shows and galleries, and his work is widely collected.

Evening Son is Stuart's fifth novel and is the fourth story in the Clay Arnold series. He enjoys the role of storyteller and in examining the human conflicts inherent to good-versus-evil. His writing is intended solely as entertainment.

Stuart lives in the bucolic countryside near Greencastle, Indiana, with his partner, Marla Helton, two dogs, two cats, and nine hens.